BLUE
MURDER

Suddenly he stopped beating time. The band went on playing, but I took my chance to leap off the podium and race through the wings to the door leading on to the pierhead. I flung it open and for a moment the force of the wind took my breath away. Reeling back, I tried to adjust my vision to the darkness.

Then I saw them. Two figures struggling by the rail.

Grady had managed to get an armlock around Diamond's neck. Sea spray pounded up from below, drenching them both, and as I went towards them the entire pierhead seemed to shift beneath my feet. It was this unexpected movement that gave Diamond a chance to break free. She thrust Grady aside, throwing her against me, and turned to run. . .

Other titles in the Mystery Thriller series:

BLUE
MURDER

by
JAY KELSO
Illustrated by Steve Braund

Hippo Books
Scholastic Publications Limited
London

Scholastic Publications Ltd,
10 Earlham Street, London WC2H 9RX, UK

Scholastic Inc,
730 Broadway, New York, NY 10003, USA

Scholastic Tab Publications Ltd,
123 Newkirk Road, Richmond Hill,
Ontario L4C 3G5, Canada

Ashton Scholastic Pty Ltd,
P O Box 579, Gosford, New South Wales,
Australia

Ashton Scholastic Ltd,
165 Marua Road, Panmure, Auckland 6,
New Zealand

First published by Scholastic Publications Ltd, 1990

Text copyright © Jay Kelso, 1990
Illustration copyright © Steve Braud, 1990

ISBN 0 590 76318 0

Made and printed by Cox & Wyman Ltd, Reading, Berks
Typeset by AKM Associates (UK) Ltd, Southall, London

10 9 8 7 6 5 4 3 2 1

Chapter One

It started with a scream.

I was walking along Dunmold Esplanade at the time, walking fast to avoid being caught by a fourteen-year-old kid called Jennifer Wainwright, who was after my body. I don't know why it is I have this effect on women, because I'm not exactly the Rambo type, but it seems that tall, skinny guys with Clark Gable ears bring out their maternal instincts. I suppose I should be flattered they find me so appealing, but when it comes to fourteen-year-olds wanting to mother me I draw the line.

Luckily a thick sea mist had come up, giving me plenty of cover. I could hear her voice calling, "Mack! Mack, wait for me," but it was getting fainter by the minute. Mack is what most people call me, which suits me fine. My real name makes me cringe, so I generally try to keep it quiet. "Mack" MacBride Esq, student chef and part-time drummer, that's me in a capsule.

When I reached the ice-cream kiosk by the pier I paused to get my breath back. The calling had stopped and there was no sound of eager size fours in hot pursuit. Great, I must have shaken her off. The kiosk was shuttered, the pier entrance barred up, the esplanade deserted. But then who in their right minds would be roaming around in a thick clammy mist at 7 pm on an April evening? Dunmold-on-Sea, I have to tell you, is just about the dullest coastal resort in the entire universe. It's so dull it makes Bognor look like Las Vegas.

Then all of a sudden this woman started screaming blue murder.

Literally.

Her voice seemed to be coming from the end of the pier, but the mist made it impossible to see beyond the amusement arcade. I immediately froze, my blood sugar dropping to zero. Speaking as one who faints at the sight of tomato ketchup and closes his eyes when watching *Tom and Jerry*, I'm a fervent believer in avoiding violence at all costs. Which is why I now hesitated, debating whether or not I should leap the barrier and dash to the rescue. Chances were I'd only make a fool of myself, interfering in some trite domestic squabble.

I was still trying to rationalize my reluctance to act when the screaming stopped.

Then came a splash.

I peered through the fog to where the sea surged invisibly between the stanchions, but couldn't make out a thing. Maybe if I went closer . . .

I hurdled the railings and dropped down to the beach.

The fog was like a white fuzzy wall rearing up in front of me and the water looked cold and hostile. I felt ashamed of myself for not plunging straight into it, but I knew very well that if there was a woman out there drowning I hadn't a hope of finding her. She wasn't even shouting, which would at least have given me a clue to her whereabouts. The only sound came from the waves, gently clawing the shingle at my feet.

I stood there too long, several minutes, cursing my indecisiveness. Surely there must be something I could do – but what?

Help, I had to go for help. I stumbled back up the shingle and again attempted to vault the railings, but this time I wasn't so successful. I landed awkwardly, bruising my heel, and was still hopping around in agony when I heard footsteps. Heavy footsteps this time, not like Jennifer Wainwright's feeble patter. Suddenly this man shot past me, his legs going like pistons, his face set and glassy-eyed, not looking to right or to left. I recognized him at once. His name was Neville Brand and he was staying with his wife at our hotel.

Or, possibly, his late wife?

He hadn't seen me. I opened my mouth to call after him, then shut it again. If he knew what I'd seen – or rather heard – he might turn nasty. Better to follow at a safe distance.

I was limping painfully along the esplanade, dropping further and further behind, when I heard this familiar sound behind me, a full-throated roar moderating to a steady phut-phut as Grady O'Rourke drew alongside on her Honda. "Hello, MacBride," she called.

Now Grady O'Rourke – incidentally, her name's deceptive because her mother comes from Goa – is about the only female I can halfway stand, mainly because she doesn't have a maternal bone in her entire superfit body. Judo Black Belt, centre-forward for the Dunmold Women's F.C. and full-time engineering student, she quite reasonably regards me as an amiable wimp. That I can take. It's the Jennifer Wainwrights of this world, all winsome lisp and adoration, who get up my nose.

"Want a lift?" Grady asked.

"Yeah, home," I panted. "No, police station. No, wait . . . better make it home first, then the police station."

She stared at me. "What's up?"

"I just heard somebody murdered." I went to climb on the pillion but she held me off.

"What do you mean, you *heard* them murdered? Didn't you see anything?"

"How could I, in this mist? Grady, I don't have time for explanations. I know the bloke who did it. He's staying at our hotel. I have to get back there quickly before he does a runner."

Again I tried to get on the bike and again she pushed me back. "So where's the body?"

"In the sea."

She glanced towards the beach. I could tell she only half-believed me. This wasn't surprising: she has a very sceptical mind. In looks she's more like a boy than a girl, except for a cloud of springy black hair; but right now the hair was hidden by her crash helmet and her face looked grim and untrusting.

"His name's Neville Brand," I told her despairingly, "and he just murdered his wife."

"In that case why should he go back to the hotel? He's hardly likely to bother about his luggage. Why not straight to the railway station?"

4

"Don't ask me. But that's not where he was heading."

She thought for a second longer, then held out the spare crash helmet. "Okay, get on."

Dunmold only has one ★★★ hotel and it isn't ours. The Bellevue is a family business: Ma keeps the books, Dad acts as Head Chef and I give him a hand when I can spare the time from my catering course at the Tech College. During the holidays, like now, I was supposed to be helping him more or less full time, but the truth is we don't altogether see eye to eye over food. He belongs to the old steak-chasseur-with-buttered-broccoli school whereas I'm more *nouvelle cuisine*.

Ma was at the reception desk when I burst through the door, leaving Grady at the foot of the steps to park the Honda.

"Mr Brand," I spluttered. "Did he come back?"

"Mmm?" Preoccupied with the register, Ma didn't even bother to look up. She was wearing loads of green eyeshadow as she always does in the evenings and one of her floral tents. She's pretty colossal, the archetypal fat lady off a seaside postcard, and also pretty dynamic. Beside her Dad and I look like a couple of anaemic pipe-cleaners.

"Mr Brand," I said urgently, leaning on the desk. "Have you seen him?"

"Mmm, yes. He's in the cocktail lounge. Came in a couple of minutes ago and asked for a brandy."

I turned to look through the open door of the cocktail lounge. Neville Brand was there all right, sitting by himself in an armchair. It was hard to believe he'd just committed the foulest deed known to man. Middle-aged, balding, his only vaguely sinister feature was a little black Hitler moustache.

He could run, though. Even allowing for my limp, he must have gone like the clappers to beat me back to the hotel *and* have time to order a drink. Not surprisingly, his breathing was still fast and there was a sheen of sweat on his pale, flabby face. Yet he seemed to have himself well under control. The only real sign of stress I could detect was the way he gripped the stem of the brandy glass.

I relaxed slightly. Clearly he wasn't planning on going anywhere for the next few minutes. I turned back to Ma and muttered, "You'd better call the police."

Her eyebrows shot up. "Police?"

"Our Mr Brand has just murdered his wife."

"Oh really, Nigel!" (Well, I suppose it had to come out some time.) "If that's meant to be a joke it's in very poor taste."

"No joke. He pushed her off the pier. But I think he may have strangled her first, to judge by the screaming."

"Is that so? Well, she seems to have made a remarkable recovery." Mum leaned over the desk to gush, "Good evening, Mrs Brand. Going to join your husband for a little drink before dinner?"

I turned to stare incredulously at the woman coming out of the Ladies' Powder Room. Diet-thin, and wearing tight white cotton trousers with a mock leopard-skin top, Mrs Brand looked like a geriatric Barbie doll. Her face was a mask of make-up and her hair the metallic blonde of a nylon wig, glistening with lacquer. Glistening, but not wet. One thing for sure, she couldn't possibly have just walked out of the sea.

She nodded distantly at Ma and went into the cocktail lounge to join her husband. He glanced up as

6

she sat down and called Nick the barman over to take her order. Unsmiling, she asked him a question and he answered. Whatever he said, it didn't seem to please her but neither did it shock her, so presumably it wasn't a confession of his guilt. She just looked miserable as sin.

Mum smiled sarcastically. "You were saying?"

"Well, he pushed *somebody* off the pier. I still think you should call the police."

"Nigel, you can't go around accusing people of murder, not without proof. Whatever it was you saw —"

"Heard. These bloodcurdling screams . . ."

"Well, you always did have an over-active imagination. Be sensible: put it right out of your mind."

I gave her a withering look and turned on my now more-or-less recovered heel.

"Where are you going?" Mum screeched after me. "We're about to serve dinner. Your father needs you in the kitchen . . ."

"If you refuse to call the police," I snapped, "then I'll have to do it myself, in person."

"Don't you dare!" Moving at incredible speed for one so vast, she was round that desk in a megasecond, pursuing me to the entrance. "Nigel, I won't have you slandering our guests. Think of the business we'd lose."

"Too bad." I charged through the door, leaving it to swing back in her face, and ran down the steps.

By the time I reached the bottom, though, I was already having second thoughts. The Dunmold police tended to regard the youth of this town with some suspicion, based mainly on their entanglements with the Prothero gang. Without proof the chances of their believing my story seemed slim. They'd probably think I was trying to hoax them – or, worse, hallucinating on illegal substances. I slowed to a halt and stood chewing my cheek. As I said, my natural instinct is to stay out of trouble.

Grady was leaning casually against the Honda, her long, leather-clad legs stretched out across the pavement. "Well?" she enquired. "Did you track him down?"

"Yeah, I tracked him down all right," I said. "He's in the cocktail lounge, having a drink with his wife, cool as you please."

Grady said nothing, just waited. It's one of the things I like best about her, she knows when to keep her mouth shut.

"I'll swear I didn't imagine it," I went on, half to myself. "I'll never forget those screams and I did hear a splash. So if it wasn't his wife he pushed off the pier, who was it?"

Chapter Two

"If there is a body," Grady said the following day, "the chances are it'll drift back on the tide."

"It might just as easily be carried out to sea," I said.

"At first, perhaps. But sooner or later everything gets washed up on the beach."

I found the thought disturbing.

We were sitting in the Seagull caff on the esplanade, drinking hot gravelly chocolate. The mist had cleared, revealing the pier in all its rococo glory – peeling paintwork, oriental minarets, the lot. During the winter it was closed, to save on upkeep, but tomorrow (Friday) it would be officially re-opened for the Easter weekend. Even as we watched, Council electricians were stringing fairy lights along the length of the pier, from the amusement arcade this end to the far Pavilion.

Thinking aloud, I said, "Last night it was still boarded up. So what was Neville Brand doing there, on the wrong side of the barrier, murdering some strange woman who wasn't his wife?"

"Maybe it was a case of mistaken identity. Visibility must have been almost nil in that fog. Perhaps he thought she *was* his wife."

"And then went sprinting back to have a drink with her at the hotel?" I shook my head. "It doesn't make sense."

"He could have been giving himself an alibi." Grady tucked her thumbs inside the top of her jeans and leaned back on the chair, rocking thoughtfully. "Have you seen them since?"

"He came down to breakfast. She had hers in bed."

"How did he seem?"

"Okay. Although he didn't eat much, just buttered toast."

"Not surprising, in the circumstances. What are they doing in Dunmold, anyway?"

"Taking advantage of our bargain Easter Break, I suppose."

"You suppose, but you don't know for certain. Why not ask him?"

"I don't believe in fraternizing with the guests. Like Dad, I prefer to keep out of sight as much as possible."

Grady shrugged. "When it comes to someone you suspect of murder I'd have thought it worth making a few enquiries."

"Set myself up as a sleuth, you mean?"

"If you like."

The idea rather appealed to me. It's true it went against my policy of staying out of trouble; but the whole problem of Neville Brand still niggled. In the clear light of today I was more than half-inclined to think Ma could be right about my over-active imagination. All the same, it wouldn't hurt to do as Grady suggested and make a few enquiries, if only to ease my conscience. At least I'd be taking some sort of action.

"Okay," I said. "Maybe I will."

"Hello, Mack," piped up a voice that made my blood run cold. "Where did you get to last night? Didn't you hear me calling you?"

Jennifer Wainwright.

She was hovering by my left elbow. Behind her, licking an ice-cream, stood her carrot-haired crony, Noella Spink. I closed my eyes and quietly groaned.

"It was awful misty," Jennifer lisped. "I couldn't see where I was going. Then someone came running and knocked me over. Look, I hurt my knee."

I glanced down at her bared knee, slightly grazed, then at her face. She must have been at her mother's make-up bag because her eyelids were caked with silver glitter and her mouth painted horror-movie red. "Who knocked you down?" I asked. "Did he have a moustache?"

"I don't know. I didn't see his face. But he smelt funny."

"How do you mean, funny?"

She wriggled. "Just . . . funny."

Grady and I exchanged a look. As a witness for the prosecution Jennifer Wainwright was clearly a dead loss.

"Ma-a-ack," she said, on three plaintive notes. "There's a disco Saturday night at the Pink Flamingo. Are you going?"

She was still holding up her skirt for me to see her knee, or maybe it was the whole podgy little leg I was meant to be admiring. "No, I shan't," I growled, "and neither should you. It could easily turn into a

11

rough house and you'd be far safer at home."

She pulled her mouth into a grimace that was possibly intended to be a sexy pout. "I can't stay home on a Saturday night. I want to have fun."

"Fun?" I said cynically. "You may get more fun than you bargained for if you go to the Pink Flamingo." Turning to Grady I murmured, "Let's get out of here," and rose to my feet.

Jennifer pursued us to the door. "Will you be home tonight if I call round?"

"No."

"But your mum said —"

"I don't care what my mother said. She knows nothing about my private life." I added sternly, "And if you'll take my advice you'll go and wash that gunk off your face before somebody gets the wrong idea."

"But I thought you'd like it . . ."

"Well, I don't. It makes you look like a Christmas tree."

She blinked at me, silver glitter ominously moist.

"Oh, heck!" I muttered, and blundered through the door, followed by Grady.

By the time we reached the Honda she was openly grinning.

"It's all very well for you," I seethed. "You don't know what it's like to be a sex object."

"No, thank the Lord. But weren't you being a little over-protective, trying to stop her going to that disco? Why not let her take her chance?"

"Grady, she's only fourteen. You know what the Pink Flamingo's like. If she gets caught up with the Prothero gang . . ." I left the rest to her imagination.

"You worry too much about the Prothero gang," she said contemptuously. "They don't scare me. Bill and Georgie are just like their father, all muscle and very little brain."

"Their father's in Parkhurst," I pointed out.

"Exactly. If he'd had more brain he wouldn't have got caught." She climbed on to the Honda and jammed the crash helmet down over her hair. "Your little groupie did say one interesting thing, though, about the guy who knocked her over. Who was, presumably, your Mr Brand."

"You mean about his smelling funny? I don't see what that tells us. Could have been anything – booze, pot, cheesey socks . . . Anyway, I didn't notice he had a funny smell."

"Maybe you didn't get so close to him as she did." Grady kicked the engine into snorting life. "I've got a judo class up at the Fitness Centre. Want to go anywhere in that direction?"

"No, thanks. I said I'd give Dad a hand in the kitchen this morning. Looks like it's going to be a busy weekend. Heyup!" I grabbed her arm. "See that woman going through the turnstile, the one in the pink fur coat? That's Mrs Brand. Now why on earth should she be taking a turn round the pier today, before anything's open?"

"Perhaps she likes fresh air," Grady said. "Or she could be visiting the scene of her husband's crime, out of morbid curiosity."

"But that would mean he's told her about it. Unless it's pure coincidence." I went on staring after the now-vanished figure in pink.

Grady gave me a prod. "Follow her."

"I can't. I promised Dad —"

"Go on, Mack, follow her. This is more important."

She was right, of course. In any case my

13

momentary hesitation was cut short by the sight of Jennifer Wainwright and Noella Spink emerging from the caff behind us. As soon as they saw me they nudged each other and started snickering behind their hands. I muttered to Grady, "See you later," and tore across the road to the pier entrance.

It wasn't hard to track down Mrs Brand. She was the only female in sight tottering up the pier in spindly high heels and a pink fur coat. Come to that, she was the only female in sight. Apart from the electricians hanging the fairy lights and a bloke putting up a sign over the fortune-teller's booth – Dunmold prides itself on preserving these archaic sideshows – the pier was deserted.

She seemed to be heading straight for the far end. Her pace was brisk, until the pier itself slowed her down. Some of the planks had rotted, leaving lethal gaps between the boards just the right size for snaring heels. After she'd turned her ankle a couple of times she proceeded with more caution, giving me a chance to catch up.

When she reached the domed edifice known as the Pier Pavilion she hesitated, as if wondering whether or not to go in. In fact the door was open, which suggested people might be working inside, getting it ready for use over the weekend. Once, in its heyday, the Pavilion had been a flourishing theatre, with a resident concert party and occasional Big Names making a guest appearance on Sundays. These days it was mainly used for Bingo, local talent contests and Oxfam fashion shows.

But Mrs Brand didn't go in. She turned instead to lean over the railings and stare out to sea. It occurred to me that where she was standing might be the very place her husband had pushed the body of his victim

14

into a watery grave. I came out in goose-bumps all over and started to back away, hoping she wouldn't see me.

Then somebody called "Di baby!" and she swung around, her expression changing swiftly from sourness to pleasure as her eyes lit on the man coming out of the Pavilion.

Built like a world heavyweight, with black crinkly hair glistening with grease, he was instantly recognizable as Ernie Prothero, uncle to the aforementioned Bill and Georgie. Also town councillor, Chairman of the Entertainments Committee and proprietor of the Pink Flamingo Club, with fingers in more pies than you can buy at Sainsbury's. Smarter and wilier than his brother George – which is probably why George was languishing in Parkhurst and Ernie was still outside.

I watched in amazement as Mrs Brand flung her arms around him. Not only, it seemed, did Neville Brand have assignations on the pier, but his wife went in for them as well. Except that in her case it took place in broad daylight and was clearly a more amicable affair than her husband's had been last night.

When they'd finished hugging they both stepped back and gazed at each other as if they hadn't met for yonks. "Great to see you, Di," Ernie Prothero said warmly. "Sorry I couldn't be around to welcome you last evening, but I had a meeting at the Town Hall. Entertainments sub-committee. Where's Neville?"

"I left him at the hotel, making some phone calls." She slipped her arm through his. "It was good of you to fix this up for us, Ernie."

"My pleasure. Let's go inside." As they moved towards the Pavilion he must have spotted me out of

15

the corner of his eye, because he swung around and snapped, "What are you doing here, MacBride? Don't you know the pier's still closed?"

"Er – no, sir. Sorry, sir."

Mrs Brand glanced at me casually. If she recognized me from the hotel lobby she gave no sign.

"You're trespassing," Ernie snarled. "Bug off."

"Yessir." Although my instinct was to run like hell – the Protheros always had that effect on me – I managed to retain at least a shred of dignity by walking collectedly back up the pier. I even made a show of nonchalance by stopping to read the sign saying *Fortunes Told, Horoscopes Cast, Palms Read, Consult Madame Olga*, but when I dared to glance over my shoulder I saw there was no point. Ernie Prothero and Mrs Brand had disappeared into the Pavilion.

The connection between them intrigued me. Nonetheless Mrs Brand wasn't my prime quarry. So her husband had stayed at the hotel to make some phone calls? It might be useful to discover to whom and about what.

I hoofed it back to the Bellevue, vaguely aware that I was being shadowed by two undersized, giggling nymphets who must have been lurking in wait for me to come off the pier. Right now, though, I had more important things on my mind.

Chapter Three

Just my luck, Ma happened to be manning the desk while the receptionist took a coffee break. "What do you mean, help out on the switchboard?" she demanded. "The kitchen's where you're needed, right this minute."

"I only thought, if guests were making a lot of calls—"

"Nigel, we do not at present have a lot of guests. Therefore they are not making a lot of calls. I'm perfectly capable of coping, thank you."

"But if there's a rush—"

"I shall hang out the flags and sing Jerusalem. Now will you please—" She broke off as someone approached and she switched on her professional smile. "Yes, Mr Brand, how can I help you?"

So he wasn't on the telephone, he was here in the lobby. Neville Brand, pusher-of-women-off-piers, was standing about a metre away from me, clutching a document case. I stared at him, fascinated, trying to

17

make out his expression, but he had the sort of closed-in, boarded-up face that gave nothing away.

"I was wondering," he said, "if you have a piano?"

Nothing fazed Ma. "Yes, of course. You'll find it in the banquetting room. It's used mainly for functions, but there's nothing booked for today, so please do avail yourself."

"Thanks," he said. "Where . . . ?"

"My son will take you. Nigel, show Mr Brand to the piano."

As we set off across the lobby I remembered what Jennifer Wainwright had said about him smelling peculiar and inclined my nose in his direction, but all I got was a strong whiff of cheap aftershave.

What Ma grandly called the banquetting room wasn't all that big, just about adequate for a medium-sized wedding reception. It had a wooden floor, tacky velvet curtains, trestle tables stacked up against the wall, and a baby grand piano.

"It's not very good," I warned him. "I don't think it's been tuned for months."

He lifted the lid and struck middle C. "Years, more likely. Never mind, I only want to go through these arrangements, make a few changes." He unzipped his document case and took out a sheaf of handwritten music.

Now if you'd asked me to make a guess at his profession, "musician" would have been about the last thing to spring into my mind. A civil servant maybe, or a secondhand car salesman; or even, with that moustache, a traveller in ladies' underwear. But a musician, never.

I was on the point of declaring my own musical interests, perhaps even telling him about the sound-proof basement room where I kept my drum-kit, when he said curtly, "Thanks, you can go now."

I'd wanted to hear what he played. If it was something I could relate to, like Thelonious Monk or Jelly Roll Morton, I could forgive him almost anything, even murder. But clearly he'd no intention of starting while I was still in the room, so I was forced to leave him to it.

Once outside, I put my ear to the door and listened. He struck a few chords and then stopped. A few more chords and silence again. Maybe he couldn't play at all? Maybe it was just a front, something to divert attention from what he was really here for . . .

"Nigel, your father's still waiting." Massive arms akimbo, Ma loomed at the far end of the passage like some vengeful Fate. I beat a tactical retreat to the kitchen.

Dad was slamming pastry lids on Dutch apple pies, always our most popular dessert. "Oh, there you are, Nige," he said. "Give Tony a hand with the veg, will you? Chop some carrots."

Tony was the commis-chef, prematurely bald and glum-looking, as you'd expect of someone who spent most of his life washing slugs off lettuce leaves. I donned my whites, equipped myself with a sharp knife and set to work.

Unfortunately the preparation of carrots is yet another area of *haute cuisine* where Dad and I disagree. He likes them sliced, I prefer them slivered. I was aware of him sending me critical glances and knew that any minute now he was going to say something, so it was partly to divert him that I asked, "Dad, you know the Brands?"

"The Brands?"

"He's called Neville and has a little black moustache." I was taking a gamble that Ma hadn't

19

mentioned my murder accusation of last evening. She and Dad are usually so whacked when they finish work that they crash straight out without saying much, and by this morning she'd probably forgotten about it. "His wife looks like she's swallowed a sackful of lemons," I added. "I think she's called Diana."

"Diamond." Dad stopped crimping pie edges to stare thoughtfully into space. "Diamond Jones, that's her professional name. Singer. Used to be quite well-known a few years back. I think she was even on *New Faces*, with the rest of the band."

"What band?"

"The Blue City Swingers. Her husband's the leader. They're appearing at the Pavilion Sunday night. Special Easter attraction." Dad wasn't being sarcastic. He sounded quite admiring of Diamond Jones and the Blue City Swingers, which suggested they weren't likely to be my cup of Earl Grey, musically speaking.

"So where's the rest of the band?" I enquired.

"Arriving Saturday, I think. Or maybe Sunday. Your mother knows." Dad went back to his crimping.

"That would explain," I mused aloud, "why I saw Mrs Brand today outside the Pavilion. She was talking to Ernie Prothero."

"Well, she would be. He's her brother."

"Her *brother*?" I froze in mid-sliver.

"That's right. She left home years ago, before you were born. Couldn't get away from Dunmold quickly enough and has hardly ever been back since. Ashamed of her roots, I shouldn't wonder." He glanced at my stationary knife. "Do get a move on, Nige. We've a party of ten coming in for lunch. Building Society's having an office shindig."

One thing about slivering carrots, it leaves your mind free to operate elsewhere. So the Brands had a Prothero connection? That opened up a whole new can of worms. And the fact I'd overheard Mrs Brand thanking her brother for fixing them up with a gig over Easter suggested they must be pretty desperate for work. No musician with a reputation worth worrying about would be grateful for a booking in Dunmold.

It also provided, I suddenly realized, a reason for Neville Brand being on the end of the pier last night. He could have been taking a look at the venue, checking the sound equipment – or rather the lack of it – and generally getting the feel of the place. But who else had been there? Who had he met?

"Dad," I said, "you haven't heard of anyone gone missing, have you? A woman."

"No, I haven't." He slung the pies on a tray and carried them over to the oven. "What do'you think I am – the Salvation Army?"

Tony said mournfully, "My Auntie Olive didn't come home last night."

I turned to stare at him. Normally he was so quiet you forgot he was there.

"But she could have been out communing with the stars," he went on. "She's done that once or twice before. It's her way of preparing herself."

"Preparing herself for what?" I enquired, only slightly curious. Tony's Aunt Olive was a weird old duck known to dabble a bit in the occult.

"Opening her booth over Easter. She gets quite nervous beforehand. She's retired now, you see. She's afraid she might be out of practice."

I felt as if someone had just clobbered me with an armoured fist. Of course! Tony's Aunt Olive was a part-time fortune-teller, otherwise known as Madame Olga – that very same fortune-teller who was billed to appear over Easter on the pier.

ON THE PIER!

I gripped Tony's arm so hard he winced. "Have you reported that she's missing?"

"Of course not." He gave me a puzzled look. "I told you, she's done this before. Auntie Vera says it's nothing to worry about."

Auntie Vera was Tony's other aunt. The two old spinsters shared a 'thirties bungalow in a cul-de-sac on the outskirts of town.

"Where does your Auntie Olive go to do this communing?" I demanded. "Would she do it on the end of the pier, for example?"

"She might. I don't know." He pulled his arm away from me and rubbed it resentfully. "Anyway, I expect she's back by now."

"Hadn't you better make sure? Give your Auntie Vera a ring." I unhooked the receiver from the wall and handed it to him.

Tony looked uncertainly at Dad.

"Oh, for heaven's sake," Dad said impatiently. "Do as he says and then maybe we can restore some sanity around here."

Tony wiped his hands, took the receiver from me and dialled a number. The conversation went something like this:

"Hello, Auntie. I just rang to ask . . . Oh . . . Oh, I see . . . No . . . Right . . . Okay . . . Yes . . . Goodbye." He hung up.

"Well?" I queried.

"No, she's not back yet. But Auntie Vera says not to worry, she's probably gone away for a while."

"Great," said Dad. "Now we've got that sorted out

maybe we can . . . Nigel, where are you going?"

By this time I'd stripped off my whites and was halfway out of the door. "Sorry," I muttered. "Something just came up."

"NIGEL . . .!"

As I cantered through the lobby Ma spotted me. "Oh Nigel, that nice little Jennifer Wainwright was here, asking for you . . ."

"Tell her to go play with her rattle." I growled.

Ma looked annoyed. "I'll thank you to remember that her father happens to be our wholesale meat supplier."

Shocked, I paused by the door. "You're surely not suggesting I should sell myself for a side of New Zealand lamb? That's immoral."

"Don't be silly." She raised her voice as I started to push my way out. "I told her to wait for you at the front of the steps."

I reversed back into the lobby.

Ma smiled grimly. "Now perhaps you'll return to the kitchen."

"Sorry, I can't." Ignoring her protests, I continued my way down the passage and out of the side entrance.

The Fitness Centre is a place I normally wouldn't be seen dead in. It has a dance studio, a gymnasium and assorted torture chambers where you can be pummelled, fried under sun lamps or merely boiled alive. The only reason I risked entering its sadistic portals was that I wanted to catch Grady at the end of her judo class. I had to tell her what I'd discovered; that there *was* a moman missing – a woman, moreover, who was a more-than-likely victim for Neville Brand to have bumped off.

Sickening noises came from inside the gym – martial cries followed by the heavy thud of flesh on rubber mat. I glanced at my watch. The class was due to finish in about ten mintes. Propping myself against the painted brick wall of the corridor, I settled down to wait.

Suddenly the outside door burst open and in walked the Prothero gang.

Chapter Four

Wild Bill Prothero, wearing the battered white stetson that gave him his nickname, was first through the door as usual, followed by his brother, Gormless George Junior, and his cousin Kevin the Kid. Now Kevin, only son of Ernie Prothero, is the one I really dislike. Wild Bill's nasty, brutish and short-tempered and Gormless Georgie has a repulsive line in whiteheads, but Kevin's mean as a hungry ferret. As soon as he saw me his shifty black eyes lit up with sadistic anticipation.

"Well, well, well," he drawled, "if it isn't Dunmold's answer to Delia Smith."

"So it is." Wild Bill hunched his shoulders a couple of times, flexing his pectorals. "I hope you baked some nice little fairy cakes, MacBride, specially for us?"

Gormless Georgie sniggered.

They advanced on me, exuding menace. To say that my stomach sank would be like saying that the

Titanic had a slight brush with an iceberg. I tried to look unconcerned, but my mouth had gone dry and my palms were sweating.

"Come for a work-out in the gym?" Wild Bill demanded, shoving his face up close to mine. His breath smelled of onions – surely only the Protheros would eat onions for breakfast? – but I dared not turn away in case he took offence. "Well, you're in luck. We'll give you a work-out you've never had before. Right, boys?"

"Right, Bill," agreed Gormless Georgie.

"Better go steady," Kevin warned.

Wild Bill looked as surprised by this as I was. "Steady?"

"Got someone special, hasn't he, staying at his crummy hotel? Special guest." When both his cousins still looked blank Kevin supplied, "Our Aunt Diamond."

"Aunt Diamond – that's right!" Wild Bill seized the front of my shirt and screwed it into a ball under my chin. Although no taller than I was – possibly half a head shorter – he was twice as wide and had hands like two clusters of Walls' prime sausages. "Hear that, MacBride? You got our Aunt Diamond staying at your hotel. She's a famous lady . . ."

"Famous singer," put in Gormless Georgie.

"Needs looking after. Good service. Good food . . ."

"None of your usual muck," leered Kevin.

"Don't want her poisoned. Get the message?"

I gritted my teeth. "She'll be treated same as our other guests, same food, same service . . ."

"Not good enough." Wild Bill gave my shirt another twist. "Not good enough for our Aunt Di."

"She's a princess," said Gormless Georgie. "Least, that's what Uncle Ernie calls her."

"Mind you," Kevin added slyly, "you can do what you like to her old man. You can put arsenic in his coffee if you want and do us all a favour."

Wild Bill grinned, relaxing his hold a little. As soon as my windpipe was free I found the courage to ask, "Why, what've you got against him?"

For a moment they looked nonplussed, then Gormless Georgie muttered, "Uncle don't like him. Says he's not good enough for Aunt Di."

"He's a musician," Kevin growled. "Everyone knows you can't trust musicians."

This may have been a snide dig at me, but I chose to ignore it. "Is that why you don't want them staying at your place? I wondered why they'd been farmed out at our hotel."

Wild Bill's expression grew even uglier than usual. "You criticizing us, saying we're not hospitable?"

"Not exactly." I started to slide along the wall towards the exit. "I just thought there might be some reason you don't want too much contact with them. Something they'd done . . ."

A large arm shot out, barring my way. "What's that supposed to mean?"

"Nothing. Just wondering."

"Fact is," put in Gormless Georgie, "our spare room's already booked. We got a visitor coming tomorrow."

"Oh, really. Who's that?"

"None of your business, MacBride." Wild Bill leaned closer. "You're too nosey by half, I think we'd better teach you a lesson."

"Yeah, teach him to mind his own business," Kevin said, grinning.

"Yeah!" Gormless Georgie rubbed his hands together gleefully. "Let's teach him."

27

"Three against one?" Desperation made me bold. "Those are cowards' odds."

Too late I realized my words were like red rags to a bull. Wild Bill's nostrils flared dangerously. "You calling me a coward, MacBride?"

"Er, not exactly—"

I ducked as his fist swung and heard it crack against the wall. He gave a howl of pain, then threw himself against me as I tried to escape. It was like being hit by a bulldozer. I fell to the floor, flattened by his bulk, and lay there, vaguely aware of Kevin and Gormless Georgie uttering the Prothero war-cry – "Wha-hoo, Bill, let him have it where it hurts!" – as they danced around, waiting for their chance to join in.

Then, as I was preparing myself for a fresh onslaught of agony, the bulk was miraculously lifted from me and the war-cry hushed. Cautiously I raised my head from the floor to see Wild Bill with a somewhat surprised expression on his face, held in an arm-lock by a superbly confident Grady O'Rourke. Behind her, ranged in an inscrutable oriental phalanx, stood her pupils from the judo class. Legs in baggy white trousers planted firmly apart, arms folded across their wrap-around shirts, they needed only her word to swing into action. Kevin and Gormless George, not surprisingly, looked apprehensive.

I got to my feet and dusted down my jeans, giving myself time to recover my equilibrium, then said conversationally, "Well, that seems to have evened up the odds a bit."

Wild Bill snarled, "Trust you, MacBride, to hide behind a woman!" He struggled to free himself, then gave a strangled yelp as Grady tightened her grip around his neck.

"Keep still," she muttered menacingly in his ear, "you little male chauvinist piglet."

"Now, Bill," I continued, "what were we talking about? Oh yes, your Aunt Diamond. Well, I'm going to make you guys a promise. From now on I'll be keeping a very close watch on your aunt – and on your Uncle Neville. In fact you can rest assured they'll have all my attention."

Another squeeze from Grady and he croaked out something that sounded suspiciously like, "Thanks."

Already Kevin and Gormless Georgie were making fast for the now-empty gymnasium. Grady released her hold on Wild Bill, at the same time raising her foot to give him a sharp boost on the rump. He half-ran, half-fell through the open door.

"Okay, class over." She dismissed her pupils with a nod and they broke ranks, dispersing to the changing rooms.

When they'd gone I said as casually as possible, because I knew she'd hate gratitude, "Good thing you were around. For a moment there I thought my end had come. What a way to go, pulverized by a Prothero!"

She slung a towel round her neck. "Why are you here, Mack? I thought you despised fitness."

"So I do. But there've been developments. Several developments, to be exact." I glanced uneasily at the gymnasium door, which was still ajar. "I'd prefer to talk elsewhere, if you don't mind."

"All right. Wait for me outside."

I found the Honda in the car park and sat on it until she reappeared, in jeans and denim jacket. While she packed her judo kit behind the saddle I told her first about Mrs Brand having been born a Prothero.

"I gathered that," she said. "But is it significant?"

"What do you mean, is it significant?" I demanded. "Of course it's significant! Where there are Protheros there's always trouble, you know that as well as I do."

"There's never been murder, though. They've never gone as far as that before."

"You mean they've never been caught."

She gave me a doubtful look. "Sometimes, Mack, I think you're paranoid where the Protheros are concerned. In this case they're not even directly involved. It's Neville Brand you suspect of murder and he isn't one of the family."

"He is by marriage. And there's another thing . . ." I told her about Tony's missing Aunt Olive.

She still looked doubtful. "Bit of a long shot, isn't it?"

"Perhaps. But the fact that she could have been on the pier last night is surely more than just coincidence."

"Communing with the stars seems a pretty harmless occupation." Grady started strapping on her crash helmet. "Why should it make Neville Brand want to push her into the sea?"

"Could have been a whim. Perhaps he has homicidal tendencies. He might even be one of those people affected by the moon."

Grady sighed. "Okay, get on. I suppose we'd better go straight there." She handed me the spare crash helmet.

"Straight where? You don't know where I want to go."

"Yes, I do. You want to visit Tony's Aunt Vera, to see if she knows anything."

"You're amazingly astute," I said, and climbed on behind her.

No 8, Wisteria Close was badly in need of a lick of paint. Weeds choked the garden and even the gnomes looked depressed. I rang the doorbell and waited.

Nobody came.

I made a helpless gesture at Grady, who was parked outside the gate. She pointed to a downstairs window and I glanced round just in time to see a net curtain falling into place. I rang again.

Shuffle, shuffle, rattle, snick. The door opened a crack, as far as the chain would allow, and a rheumy blue eye peered out at me suspiciously. "Yes?"

I thought I'd better establish my credentials as quickly as possible. "Hello, Miss Pilling. My name's MacBride and I'm a friend of your nephew Tony. I was wondering if—?"

"Is he all right?" The blue eye widened in alarm. "There's not been an accident?"

"No, he's fine. I came about your sister—"

"She isn't here." The door started to close.

"Yes, I know. Tony told me. He—"

Too late. The door had slammed shut.

I bent down to peer through the letter-box. "Miss Pilling? Miss Pilling, are you still there? I only wanted to ask—"

"Go away!" A pair of furry pink mules did an agitated dance on the doormat. "Leave me alone. It's nothing to do with me."

"What's nothing to do with you?"

"I don't know. I don't know anything about it. *Go away!*"

The sharp end of an umbrella came poking through the letter-box, narrowly missing my eye. I jumped back hastily. Clearly the old dear was scared out of her wits and I was only making things worse. If I wanted to question her I'd have to adopt a more subtle approach, through Tony for example. "Okay," I called, backing away. "It's okay, I'm going."

By the time I reached the gate Grady was already revving the engine. Before I had time to tell her what happened she rapped out, "Get on, quick."

"Why, what's the hurry?"

"Don't argue, get on."

I got on and was still fastening my crash helmet when she took off, nearly unseating me. "What's up?" I demanded of her left ear.

"Parked car," she threw over her shoulder as she swung into a U-turn. "Other side of road. Watching."

I'd already seen it, out of the corner of my eye, a dark blue Mercedes that could only belong to one person. As we sped past I spotted, through heavily tinted windows, the ominous bulk of Ernie Prothero.

Chapter Five

"What do you make of it?" I asked when we stopped on the esplanade, a couple of hundred metres from the Bellevue.

Grady said she couldn't think on an empty stomach, so we bought a couple of hot dogs at a mobile stall and sat in a nearby shelter to eat them, facing the sea. The shelter stank like a public loo and was littered with empty 7-Up cans, but at least we had all-round vision, albeit through murky glass, and could therefore talk without fear of being overheard. Grady's accusation of paranoia might have had some truth in it, but it certainly seemed to me that Protheros were popping up all over the place these days.

"Do you think Ernie recognized us?" I asked.

Grady shrugged. "Why should he? He probably doesn't even know who we are."

"He knows who I am. He called me by my name this morning on the pier."

"Don't forget you were wearing a crash helmet by the time we passed him. Everyone looks different in a crash helmet."

I found this only moderately comforting. "Was he there when we arrived? I didn't notice the car."

"No, he turned up while you were chatting on the doorstep."

"Do you think he meant to go in? Because if he does he'll get an umbrella through his eye. The old dear's scared stiff of something. I'm not sure what. She's not in a mood to talk to anyone."

Grady took a piece of gristly sausage out of her roll and chucked it at a passing seagull, who caught it adeptly while still on the wing. "It looked to me as if he was content to sit there and wait."

"Wait for what? What was he expecting to see?"

She didn't even attempt to answer.

I stared out to sea, which was a lot more active than it had been last night, whipped up by a fresh south-easterly wind. It suddenly occurred to me that poor old Olive Pilling might be out there somewhere, being tossed around in the current, a cold and swelling corpse. It was a chilling thought.

"Supposing," I said, "just supposing that Neville Brand did tell his wife what happened on the pier . . . and that she told Ernie this morning . . . he could have gone round to the Pillings to find out if Vera knew anything . . . couldn't he?"

Grady looked dubious. "But why should Ernie worry about Neville Brand being found out? He doesn't even like the guy."

"Maybe Mrs Brand pleaded with him to help. The Protheros always stick together, they're famous for it." I swallowed the last bit of hot dog and took off down the beach to wash my hands in the sea. When I

34

returned I added, "Whichever way you look at it, Ernie's sudden interest in the Pilling sisters is pretty sinister. I think I'd better get back to the Bellevue and have another word with Tony."

"Okay." Grady stood up. "How about this evening?"

"This evening?"

"Will you be going down the town after you've finished work?"

I shook my head. "Sorry, Grade. It's Thursday."

Thursday's my jazz night. Band practice at the Dunmold Memorial Hall eight till eleven. Grady knew that, but she must have forgotten. Just for a moment her normally dead-pan face showed something like disappointment.

"Oh, yeah," she muttered. "Okay, see you."

When the Honda had gone, with an even throatier roar than usual, I walked back along the esplanade to the Bellevue. There were times, not very often, when I suspected Grady quite fancied me; but I generally dismissed the idea as unlikely. She wasn't the type – by which I mean, of course, the Jennifer Wainwright type. Heaven forbid!

By the time I got back to the Bellevue lunch was more or less over. To avoid Ma I sneaked in the side entrance to the kitchen and took a shufti through the serving hatch. The Building Society party had gone; Neville Brand sat alone in the dining-room, sipping a coffee.

"Hello, Treasure." Sandra, our longest-serving waitress, appeared on the other side of the hatch. She was fair, fat and fortyish, but still game enough to flirt. "Where've you been all my life? This lunch-time, anyroad. Your name's been mud."

"Had to go out," I muttered, peering over her

shoulder at Neville Brand. "Where's his wife?"

"Whose wife?" She glanced at the lone luncher. "Oh, you mean Hitler's. Don't ask me. She never turned up. Got other fish to fry, I expect. Can't say I blame her. He's a gloomy devil."

"He's probably got a lot on his mind," I understated.

"How about you, Mack?" Sandra leaned further through the hatch to tweak my chin. "You got things on your mind?"

"Yeah," I growled. "Like murder."

She visibly recoiled. Behind her Neville Brand pushed away his coffee cup, stood up and walked over to the exit. I dodged back, out of his sight, and cannoned into Dad.

"Well, if it isn't the Prodigal returned," he said. "Nice of you to show up, son. Sure you can spare the time?"

I offered, as a penance, to help Tony prepare the salads. He accepted.

As soon as Tony and I were alone in the kitchen I asked, "Any news yet of your Aunt Olive?"

He gave me a look that was both puzzled and guilty. "I don't know, Mack. You think it's serious?"

"Could be. Perhaps you ought to check." I jerked my head towards the telephone.

He hesitated. "I don't want to worry Auntie Vera . . ."

"She's already worried," I said. "This morning I passed by her bungalow and saw her on the doorstep. She looked worried to death."

This was no more than the truth. I only hoped it wouldn't strike Tony as odd that I should be passing by in a cul-de-sac.

"I think," I prompted, "you should call again."

"Okay." He wiped his hands on the towel with great thoroughness and went over to the telephone. Tony did everything in slow motion. Sometimes he drove Dad mad, he took such an age to do the smallest job: but you always knew the job would be done well, provided you didn't mind waiting.

He picked up the receiver and carefully dialled the number. After a few seconds he put the receiver down again. "Line's busy."

"What do you mean, busy? Engaged?"

He nodded. "I'll try again later."

"Maybe you should go round there, check she's okay?"

"Maybe I will," he agreed. "After I've finished work."

It was useless trying to hustle him. I could hardly tell him the truth, that I suspected one of his old aunts had been murdered and the other was in mortal danger, because I knew he wouldn't believe me. Such things didn't happen in Dunmold. At least, not in Tony's Dunmold.

When I finally emerged from the kitchen Ma was lurking at the far end of the passage. Instinctively I took evasive action, but just as instinctively she turned around to catch me dodging into a doorway and called, "Nigel, come here!"

Reluctantly I obeyed. But when I got closer I saw that her expression was surprisingly honey-sweet and realized she was not alone. Her companion was Neville Brand.

"Nigel," she cooed, "I've just been telling Mr Brand that you're a musician. Only an amateur, of course, but quite accomplished. He said he'd like to meet you."

I found this hard to believe, especially as he was

looking at me like a food inspector faced with a bad case of botulism.

"Drums, is it?" His tone was gruff, almost aggressive. "Got your own kit, I hear?"

"Down in the basement," Ma chipped in. "We had the room sound-proofed, so the guests aren't disturbed."

Neville Brand didn't even look at her. "Ever played with a band?"

"Yeah," I drawled, determined not to be patronized. "With the Dunmold Youth Jazz Band, as a matter of fact. We're twenty-five strong."

Which made us, at a guess, considerably stronger than the Blue City Swingers.

"They've won prizes," Ma added, "at the County Music Festival."

He looked impressed. "Practice regular?"

Ma answered for me. "Every Thursday night, at the Memorial Hall, eight o'clock."

"That's tonight." He stroked his moustache. "Might come and give you an ear. Be okay if I do?"

"Yeah, of course." I tried not to show how totally pole-axed I was by this show of interest in my musical talent. Why in the name of Jelly Roll Morton should he want to come and hear a gang of kids play jazz? And not even, I suspected, his kind of jazz.

Ma beamed at him. "That's really nice of you, Mr Brand. Nigel would be thrilled if you went to hear him play. Wouldn't you, Nige?"

I tried to look thrilled. Most likely I just looked sick.

Mr Brand nodded. "Okay. No promises, mind. But I'll see if I can fit it in."

As he walked away from us I felt a surge of resentment. Who did he think he was, acting like some grand international impresario instead of a tin-pot little dance-band leader so down on his uppers he was grateful for a gig on Dunmold Pier?

"There now," Ma said triumphantly. "A contact like that, you never know where it might lead."

I didn't bother to argue. In any case it seemed wise to fade away while she was still in a good mood. I went back to the kitchen and did a little extra penance by scrubbing down single-handed.

The main reason why the Dunmold Youth Jazz Band held its practices in the Memorial Hall was that there weren't too many houses close by, and, provided doors and windows were kept shut, the noise level was just about within the legal limit.

Most of us had started playing at school, under the direction of Harry (Flash) Gordon, who taught all kinds of music but was a jazz fanatic. It was he who'd developed our talent and our tastes, knocked us into some sort of musical shape and was ultimately responsible for our modest but notable success. He was a tough man to please, but when Flash muttered, "Now we're getting somewhere", as he occasionally did, the entire band swelled with pride.

I warned him, before we started, that we might have a visitor. "Sorry, Flash, but it was hard to say no, considering he's a guest at our hotel."

Flash grinned. For a schoolteacher he cut a pretty colourful figure in a mustard shirt with a red bow tie worn not at his throat but at the nape of his neck, to hold back his long grey hair. "Let him come. Might even teach him a thing or two. Open his eyes."

"Might," I agreed, unconvinced. "Although I think this guy's got his eyes shut tight. Probably tone deaf as well."

"Most band leaders are."

This exchange made me feel better. All musicians are notoriously intolerant of each other's music, but siding with Flash gave me confidence. It even affected my playing. I beat the living daylights out of the bass drum that night, thinking of the Prothero gang; bashed the hi-hat cymbal metaphorically down over Ernie's head; and tickled the snare with enough panache to make mincemeat of Neville Brand. The music absorbed my entire concentration, and I was only vaguely aware of a shadowy figure lurking in the dark recesses of the hall.

The knowledge that he was there, and listening, and possibly being favourably impressed, gave me some satisfaction.

It also made me a little uneasy.

Chapter Six

Next morning, while I was still on breakfasts, Tony came in. "Any news?" I enquired.

He looked a little shamefaced. "I did try to call again last night, but there still wasn't any reply. I think her phone must be out of order."

Grimly I took the frying-pan off the heat and went to lift the receiver from the hook. "What's her number?"

He told me and I rang it. All I got was a continuous high-pitched whine.

"See what I mean?" Tony said gloomily.

I replaced the receiver. "Sounds like she's been cut off. Come on."

"Come on where?"

"Up to your Auntie Vera's, of course." I stripped off my whites and threw them over a chair. Dad appeared from the deep-freeze just as we were going through the door, but before he could open his mouth I told him, "Emergency. Old lady in trouble," and yanked Tony out of the kitchen by his arm.

We caught a Dunmold Rover, one of the toy-sized boneshakers run by the local bus company, to the outskirts of town and walked the rest of the way to Wisteria Close. Tony was clearly mystified by my concern for his maiden aunt and I made no attempt to enlighten him. When we neared the cul-de-sac I slowed down, just in case a Prothero-style Mercedes was parked anywhere near, but there were only a few nondescript cars and one small white van.

The bungalow looked more forlorn than ever. All the windows were closed and the curtains drawn. I had a cold, sinking sensation in the pit of my stomach.

Tony rang the bell. As before, nobody answered. He rang twice more and nothing happened. I began to curse myself for not taking action sooner. I should have made Tony come yesterday, instead of waiting another twenty-four hours. The poor old dear was probably lying on the floor by now with the telephone cord round her neck.

Tony stepped back and yelled, "Auntie! Auntie, are you there?"

A curtain twitched.

"It's me – Tony. I've come to see if you're okay."

The curtain moved again and Vera Pilling's ghostly face looked out fearfully; but when she saw who it was she mouthed something at us, possibly "Wait there", and disappeared. A few minutes later the door was opened, still with the chain on.

"Tony, you alone?"

"No, I've got a friend with me. Mack from the hotel."

I said quickly, "We were worried about you, Miss Pilling. Is anything wrong?"

"No, why should it be?"

42

"Your phone's gone phut," Tony said. "I was trying to get you all yesterday. I wanted to know if Auntie Olive's come home."

" 'Course she came home. I said she would, didn't I?"

This news came as a distinct shock. If Olive Pilling was alive it meant I still didn't know who'd been pushed off the pier. The trouble with this murder case was that none of the likely bodies stayed dead.

"Oh, that's all right, then," Tony said with evident relief. "I was beginning to think she must have lost her memory."

"Nothing wrong with Olive's memory." Vera removed the chain and grudgingly opened the door. "You'd best come in."

We stepped into the narrow hall. It smelled of cats and stewed rhubarb. Vera pushed us into the sitting-room.

"Why are the curtains drawn?" Tony asked.

"Haven't had time to open them yet." Vera padded, in her furry pink mules, over to the window to pull back the mud-coloured dralon, but only halfway. Light filtered through festooned nets to show a small room crammed with dark brown furniture. It also showed Vera Pilling, scrawnier and sourer than her sister. Olive was really rather a nice old duck, the sort that keeps a packet of soft-centred mints in her handbag to dish out to other people's kids. I was glad she hadn't been bumped off, even if it did make a nonsense of my theory.

"So where is Auntie Olive?" Tony enquired, looking round. In fact the sole occupant of the room was a large ginger tom, curled up in the best armchair and blinking in the light.

"Gone away," said Vera.

43

"I thought you said she came back?"

"So she did. Now she's gone again."

Tony looked mystified, as well he might. "Where to?"

"Brighton, probably. Got an old schoolfriend lives there. Phoebe James. I daresay she's gone to visit her."

"But it's Easter," I said. "What about her booth on the pier?"

"Yes, well . . . she decided against it. You get funny people on piers nowadays. Some folk turn quite nasty after they've had their palms read if they don't like what they hear."

Had Neville Brand turned nasty? While Tony went on talking to his aunt I noticed the telephone, the old-fashioned kind with a dial, on a table beside the fireplace. On the pretext of stroking the cat, I bent to inspect the cord.

It had been cut. The end dangled useless beside the socket.

At the same moment I distinctly heard a noise coming from another room, like a creaking floorboard or maybe a door. But before I could say anything the cat turned on me with a yowl and bit my wrist.

"Should have warned you," Vera said with a grim satisfaction. "He don't like being stroked."

The pain distracted me, leaving only half my brain free to make sense out of what I'd seen and heard. Nursing my wrist, I said, "Your telephone—"

"It's been reported. They're sending somebody round." Vera scooped up the cat and murmured in his ear, as if he were the injured party. "Did he frighten you, my precious? Never mind, he's going now." She turned to the door.

Tony followed her sheepishly. "Well, as long as you're all right, Auntie . . ."

"'Course I'm all right. Not senile yet, you know." At the front door she said, in a gentler tone, "Still, it was nice of you to come, Anthony. You're a good boy at heart."

I slid warily past the cat, still clutched to its owner's droopy bosom. As soon as I'd reached the step I said, "About your sister, did you really see her yesterday, in the actual flesh? I mean, you didn't just get a message or something?"

Vera glowered at me. "You calling me a liar?"

"No, of course not. I just—"

The door slammed in my face.

"Flaming cat!" I muttered, not necessarily meaning the ginger tom.

Tony glanced at my wrist. "Give you a nasty nip, I'll bet. You'd better wash it in disinfectant as soon as you can or you might get rabies."

I followed him down the path. "You realize there was somebody else in there? I heard them."

He said calmly, "I expect it was Mrs Grundy, who lives next door. She's always popping in."

"And the wire was cut. That's why the telephone didn't work."

"That's okay. Auntie said it was being fixed."

I closed the gate behind me, then looked up and down the road. "Tony, do you recognize these cars? I mean, are they always parked outside, or is there one you haven't seen here before."

"I don't come that often, Mack." He gave me a puzzled look. "What are you getting at?"

I hesitated to put it into words. Instead I hedged, "Only that she seemed very keen to get rid of us. And we still haven't seen your Auntie Olive. We've no real proof that she's okay."

For a moment he stared at me, then his face took on a kindly, rather pitying expression. "You know, it isn't true that the youth of today don't bother about the old folk. It's really nice the way you worry about my Auntie Olive. But you needn't, Mack, not any more. If Auntie Vera says she's okay, then she's okay, truly she is. Now we'd better get back or your father'll have our guts for sausages."

We didn't talk much on the return jouney. I don't know what Tony was thinking, but my private conviction, growing stronger by the minute, was that someone else, most likely a Prothero, had been lurking in that bungalow, threatening Vera Pilling with horrendous consequences if she talked. Why else should the telephone wire be cut from the inside?

Nor was I in the least convinced by the story that Olive had gone for a spur-of-the-moment holiday with some old schoolfriend in Brighton. No, she was still missing. My theory remained intact.

"Nigel," Ma said as soon as I emerged from the gents, where I'd been washing dried blood out of the teeth-marks on my wrist, "you're wanted in the ban-quetting room."

"Why, what's on?" I asked, trying to remember if we had anything booked, like a wedding reception or a wake. In the light of recent developments a wake seemed the more likely.

"Mr Brand's been asking for you." Ma's face was deep pink, as if she were bursting to say something but trying hard not to. "The rest of his band has arrived. They're using the banquetting room to practice in."

"Oh, I see." I glanced at the register. "Are they

staying here?"

"No, they're booked into various B & B places all over town. I daresay they can't afford our prices," Ma said loftily.

Yet Mr and Mrs Brand could? I doubted it. Likely as not Ernie Prothero was footing the bill, for his sister's sake if not for her husband's.

"Why does he want to see me?" I asked.

"I think you'd better go and find out." She reached across the desk to tweak the collar of my sweatshirt. "Make yourself look respectable, there's a good boy."

Something was definitely afoot.

Outside the banquetting room I paused to listen. Just as I'd suspected – top-heavy brass section, ropey woodwind, treacle-sweet arrangement. In other words, a skimpy line-up trying to make a Big Band sound but failing dismally, partly due to the total absence of a rhythm section. I sighed and opened the door.

Neville Brand had his back to me, facing a pretty seedy-looking group of players. None of the Blue City Swingers would see forty again, a couple were definitely OAPs. All looked as if they'd slept in their clothes and hadn't eaten properly for weeks.

"Neville!" Mrs Brand, in a low-cut black top and tight red slacks, was perched on the baby grand at the far end of the room. Her voice, full and throaty, was powerful enough to cut through the off-key brass. "Neville, the boy's here."

The music died. Neville Brand turned his head, saw me and came over. "Listen, son . . ." He put an arm around my shoulder, which I didn't much care for, in the circumstances. It could well be the arm that had shoved poor old Olive into the drink.

47

"How'd you like to earn yourself some pocket money?"

"Doing what?" I asked cautiously.

"Doing what you like best, making music." He was trying hard to be pleasant, but I refused to be won over. Even Hitler, so they said, could be charming when he'd wanted. "Fact is, we're in a bit of a hole. Our drummer hasn't turned up. Now I heard you last night, kid, and you're not bad. Seems to me you could fill in pretty well. Nothing fancy, just keeping a nice, steady tempo. Think you could do that?"

Do it? I could do it standing on my head with both feet tied together and one hand shelling peas. I did not say this aloud, however, since I was for the moment totally gob-smacked.

"Okay, let's give it a try," he said kindly. "Go fetch your drum-kit and we'll put you through your paces."

Chapter Seven

The first thing I did, as soon as I was free, was to ring Harry Gordon. I told him the situation and asked what he thought I should do.

"Take it," he said. "It'll be good experience."

"But the band – it's a real bummer, Flash."

"Son, if I had a fiver for every time I've played with a bum band I'd be a millionaire by now. Don't be such a snob, Mack. Take the money and give the gentleman what he wants, a nice gentle little background beat, no questions asked."

"It seems like prostitution . . ."

"How much is he paying you?"

"£2.50 an hour for practice and twenty-five quid for the actual performance."

"That's not prostitution, that's charity. Forget your scruples. Play."

I thanked him for his advice and hung up. I still wasn't happy; but the real reason, of course, had nothing to do with my high musical standards. It was the thought of knowingly allying myself with a murderer, actually helping him out in his hour of need. But this, of course, I couldn't explain to Harry Gordon. I wished there were someone else I could talk it over with . . .

"Ah, there you are, Nigel." Ma's voice had taken on a fondly maternal note ever since Neville Brand told her he wanted me for his band. "There's a young lady waiting to see you."

Grady! Just the person . . .

But it wasn't Grady. It was Jennifer Wainwright.

"Hello, Mack." She flapped her eyelashes, obviously false and none too secure, and smiled come-hitherishly at me.

I groaned. "Who let you in?"

"Now, Nigel," Ma said reprovingly. "That's not polite. Jennifer has something she wants to ask you."

Outnumbered, I gave up. "Okay, so what is it?"

"You remember that disco tomorrow night at the Pink Flamingo, the one I told you about? Well, I asked my mum if I could go and she said only if I went with someone who'd look after me, so I told her I might be going with you and she said that would be fine, because you were a nice boy and you came from a nice family." Here little Miss Smarmypants swivelled her black-fringed eyes round to Ma, who visibly fluffed out her feathers with pride at this unsolicited testimonial from the wife of our wholesale meat supplier.

I said firmly, "I already told you, I never go to discos. The music's naff and I don't dance."

Ma's face froze. Jennifer's eyes filled with tears.

I hardened my heart. "Sorry, but that's the way it is."

Ma said, "Nigel, I really do think—"

"Leave it out, Ma. I've got enough on my plate right now." I turned to Jennifer. "And I also said that you shouldn't go there either. The Pink Flamingo isn't the place for a kid like you. If you'll take my advice you'll keep away."

Jennifer blinked. Her lower lip trembled.

Ma said gently, "Nigel's right, dear. You're far too young to get mixed up with the sort of boys that go to the Pink Flamingo."

"Yes, Mrs MacBride," Jennifer murmured meekly. "I'd better go, then. Goodbye, Mack."

She turned and headed for the door, her shoulders drooping. As she reached it I called, "Hang on a moment. There's something I want to ask you."

She swung round, her face eager.

I went over to her, out of Ma's earshot. "You know the other night, in the fog, when that guy bumped into you – well, you said he smelled funny and I was wondering, can you remember exactly how he smelled? I mean, was it drink or cigarettes or what? Please, try to remember. It could be important."

She frowned. "Well, I think it was more like scent, really."

"Scent? You mean aftershave?"

"Sort of. But not my dad's aftershave. That's terrible, it stinks the bathroom out for hours." She frowned harder. "No, it was more like a woman's scent."

I felt a surge of triumph. If Neville Brand smelt of a woman's scent it must surely mean that it had rubbed off on him during the struggle. I wondered if Tony would be able to remember what kind of scent his Auntie Olive used? He might even have given her some for Christmas . . .

"Okay, Jennifer. Thanks." I gave the door a push,

helping her on her way, and when she'd disappeared I evaded Ma's inquisitive gaze and made straight for the kitchen.

Tony didn't know what scent Olive Pilling used. He'd never given her any for Christmas. The only smell he associated with her was peppermint and why was I so interested anyway? It was obvious that my continued curiosity about his aunt was beginning to annoy him, so I quit the hotel altogether and went down the town in search of Grady.

I found her hanging out near the new shopping mall with a gaggle of her biker cronies, mostly male. When I approached they eyed me warily, as if I were some kind of alien life form. Even Grady didn't looked all that thrilled to see me, but when I muttered, "Developments," to her, as near as possible without moving my lips, she detached herself from her bike and let me draw her into W.H. Smith's, where the general racket allowed us perfect privacy to talk.

She listened in silence while I told her first of my new engagement with the Blue City Swingers, and then of my trip with Tony to his aunts' bungalow. The news of my debut as a professional musician seemed to leave her unmoved, but when I mentioned the cars we'd seen parked in the cul-de-sac she said abruptly, "Billy Prothero runs a white van."

"He does?" I stopped flipping through the Special Offer tapes in case there were any jazz greats – there weren't – and turned to stare at her. "It could have been him, then, inside with poor old Vera."

"If it was," Grady said slowly, "I don't fancy her chances. He's the type who would beat up old ladies without a twinge of conscience. We'd better get up there right away."

Which is how, for the second time that day, I found myself outside the Pilling bungalow.

Once there, however, I felt strangely reluctant to act, despite the sinister fact of the white van being parked in exactly the same place as this morning. For one thing, my wrist still bore the faint imprint of feline teeth; and for another I could think of no good reason to offer Vera Pilling for my ongoing concern about her well being, which was beginning to border on the obsessional.

"I think we should wait and watch for a while," I said to Grady. "Make ourselves as unobtrusive as possible."

"Not easy in a cul-de-sac," she pointed out. "If we hang around we're bound to look suspicious."

"Then we'll wander down to the end of the road and take a casual look over the fence at the allotments. Nobody can object to that."

She left her bike at the side of the road and we strolled along the pavement at the hectic pace of a couple of snails. As we passed the van I glanced inside.

Five paces on I muttered, "Did you see what I saw?"

She nodded. "Someone crouching on the floor."

"It wasn't Bill. Looked more like Gormless George Junior." We reached the end of the cul-de-sac and leaned against the fence, gazing over neat rows of purple sprouting broccoli. "He must have seen us arrive."

"If Georgie's acting as look-out," Grady said, "that means it's Bill inside, just as we thought. Maybe Kevin as well."

My stomach registered acute misgiving. I continued to gaze over the allotments, seeking inspiration from the broccoli.

"If you want my opinion," Grady went on, "there's no point in our going to the bungalow. We'd only make things worse. I think our best bet is to tackle Georgie. He's the weak link in that operation. With a little gentle persuasion he might even tell us what's going on."

I'd been coming round to this idea myself. Turning my back on the allotments I said, "Okay, let's creep up on him, take him by surprise."

We strolled back the way we'd come. As we neared the car I put out a hand to stop Grady and pointed to the van's wing mirror. It reflected Gormless Georgie, now upright in the driver's seat and looking somewhat anxious. From the direction of his gaze I deduced he had his eyes fixed on Grady's Honda.

I wrenched open the door before he had time to realize what was happening and poked my head into the van. "Hi, George. Having trouble?"

He flushed puce. "What'd you mean, trouble?"

"Engine trouble. You've been stuck here all day. Anything we can do to help?"

He was silent for at least four seconds. You could tell by the way his eyebrows twitched that his brain was ticking over at what was, for him, a fantastic speed. At length he said cautiously, "Nothing wrong with the engine. I'm just keeping an eye on things, that's all."

By now Grady had moved into his line of vision. She stood, long legs placed slightly apart, hands on hips, staring at him. George shifted uneasily in his seat.

"All by yourself?" I enquired sympathetically. "Where are Bill and Kevin?"

"I dunno. Bill done the morning shift, Kevin's

coming along later." He glanced at his watch, then added ominously, "I reckon he'll be here soon."

"Shift?" I queried. "You mean you're taking it in turns?"

" 'Sright."

I straightened and exchanged a look with Grady. The chances were that Georgie was telling the truth: he didn't have the brains to lie. Which meant that Wild Bill wasn't inside the Pilling bungalow. Nor was Kevin. Their brief was merely to keep watch.

I bent down again. "Did your uncle ask you to do this?"

He glowered at me, as if realizing he might already have said too much. "What if he did?"

"I just wondered what reason he gave you. Do you have any idea *why* you're doing it?"

" 'Course I do." Suddenly he seemed more confident. "The two old girls that live in that bungalow, they haven't paid their rent for months. Uncle Ernie's getting fed up of waiting for the money, so he's told 'em straight, they gotta cough up or else. Now he's afraid they might try to do a bunk, so we're keeping an eye on 'em, round the clock, just in case." George looked pleased with himself, as if surprised he'd managed to produce such a coherent explanation.

I wasn't sure what to make of this. Tony had never mentioned that Ernie Prothero was his aunts' landlord, but that didn't mean it couldn't be true. Georgie clearly believed it. If such a thing as honesty could shine out of such a pair of shifty eyes it was shining now. But I wouldn't put it past Ernie to con even his own family into doing his dirty work for him.

I said, "So you've been watching the bungalow all day. Seen anything interesting?"

"Yeah!" George's mean little eyes grew spiteful. "I seen you, Mack. And so did Bill, he saw you this morning. It's all down here, in black and white." He pointed to a dog-eared notebook resting on the dashboard. "We been keeping a record. I reckon Uncle Ernie'll be real interested to see how often you been coming to visit."

Twice today. And what's more he'd seen me himself yesterday, when he was parked outside in his Mercedes. I muttered, "Okay, Georgie, keep up the good work," and slammed the van door shut. To Grady I hissed, "Let's go," and hustled her towards the Honda.

She asked, "Don't you want to check on Vera Pilling?"

"What's the point? There's no one inside. You heard what Georgie said."

"But how about those noises you heard – and the telephone wire?"

"She could have cut it herself, to avoid being got at by Ernie."

"You surely don't believe what Georgie said?"

"I don't know what I believe, Grady. Except that when Ernie Prothero reads what's written in that notebook I shall be a marked man."

Chapter Eight

We had a rush on for dinner that night, which meant that in the kitchen we scuttled around like demented ants. Clive, the second chef, cut his finger, one of the waitresses dropped a tray loaded with avocadoes vinaigrette and Ma kept popping her head round the door to bawl us out for slow service. The only person who stayed calm in all this was Dad. Nothing ever seemed to ruffle him, no matter what. I liked to think I took after him in this respect, but judging by the beads of sweat dripping off my brow into the soup of the day (French onion) this was probably self-delusion.

All in all, it was some time before I had a chance to ask Tony if it was true about Ernie Prothero being his aunts' landlord. He gave me a distinctly dubious look. "Why, what's it to you, Mack?"

I said frankly, "Just that I think Ernie may be up to something and I'm trying to carry out a check on his activities."

"You'd better be careful. If he finds out you've been asking questions he won't take it kindly."

Well aware how true this was, I nonetheless said, with virtuous bravado, "Somebody's got to stop him sometime, he's been getting away with things too long."

"Maybe so." Tony pulled at his long blue chin. "But fair's fair, he's always been straight in his dealings with the old girls. Auntie Olive has quite a soft spot for him."

I was about to say that buttering up old ladies was all part of Ernie's villainy, when the significance of Tony's remark hit me. So he *was* their landlord . . .

"You don't happen to know," I said, "if they've fallen behind with their rent?"

"No, I don't!" He was clearly offended. "And I don't see it's any of your business, either. Stop poking your nose in where it don't belong, Mack."

I was about to apologize when Ma appeared, resplendent in a navy tent with silver trimmings, and said, "Nigel, Mr Brand wants you in the banquetting room. He's called another practice session."

"Not another one," I groaned. "That's the second today. I thought they were supposed to be professional musicians."

"He says they haven't played together for a long time. Anyway, this one's for his wife's benefit. She wants to loosen up her vocal chords." Ma gave me a critical glare. "You look terrible, all hot and sweaty. You'd better take a shower first and put on a clean shirt."

Out of the corner of my eye I saw Tony stomping off huffily in the direction of the staff room. It seemed pointless to follow him. I vowed I'd never ask him another question about his aunts as long as I lived.

Showered and clean-shirted, I arrived in the banquetting room to find the Blue City Swingers already swinging, loudly and without much finesse. Neville Brand acknowledged my arrival with a nod and jerked his head in the direction of the podium. I picked up my drumsticks and fell into the rhythm without difficulty. After my exertions in the kitchen I found the monotonous rum-ti-ti-tum beat so soporific it was as much as I could do to keep my eyes open.

Any ideas I might have had of dozing off, however, were shattered as soon as Mrs Brand started to sing. Rightly named Diamond, she had a voice that could cut through double glazing. Waving her stringy arms around like a windmill, she belted her way through *Goldfinger*, *Hey, Big Spender* and an embarrassingly emotional rendering of *My Way*. Shirley Bassey has a lot to answer for.

When she'd finished, someone at the back of the room started to clap. I glanced at the two people standing there, and saw to my extreme dismay that one of them was Ernie Prothero. "That was great, Di," he called out, beaming all over his face with brotherly pride. "You've lost none of your old magic."

Which just goes to show how much he knew about music.

He came towards her, his arm around his female companion. "Look who I've brought to see you," he went on, ignoring Neville Brand completely. "Bet you don't recognize her. It must be years since you last met."

It was at this point that I looked properly for the first time at the girl beside him and experienced something akin to a blow on the head from a concrete pile-driver. Slender and bouncy as a dancer, and with honey-coloured hair, she looked far too young and vulnerable to be mixed up with a crook like Ernie Prothero. My Galahad streak, which I didn't even know I had, came to the fore. I wanted to leap over the brass section and snatch her out of his far-too-familiar embrace.

But then Mrs Brand said, "Of course I recognize her, it's Bonnie," and kissed the air somewhere in the region of the girl's cheek.

"Okay, take five," Neville said wearily, and wandered off to the piano where he pretended to be busy sorting out sheets of music.

By now I was frantically searching my memory for what I knew about Bonnie Prothero, the missing daughter who'd gone off with her mother when Ernie's first marriage broke up. I'd known her, of course I'd known her, when we were both at Botley Road Junior School, in Mrs Claymore's class. But she hadn't been anything out of the ordinary then, just a plain little shrimp with freckles. Now she had a bloom on her like a Grade A peach. Ye gods, she couldn't possibly be Kevin's sister, there wasn't the slightest family resemblance! She must take after her mother, whom I dimly remembered as being rather glamorous, certainly a lot better-looking than the hard-faced gypsyish woman Ernie was married to now.

"Fancy a fag?" It was the trumpet-player who spoke to me, holding out a packet of Benson & Hedges. He went by the name of Windy – Sam "Windy" Clayton – and had the look of an elderly bloodhound being put through his paces when he'd far rather be asleep on the rug.

"Thanks," I said, "but I don't smoke."

"Sensible lad. I shouldn't either, in my line of business. Still, it's not done me any harm so far." He coughed wheezily, stuck a cigarette in his mouth and lit it. "You're doing okay, son."

"Thanks," I said again, my eyes riveted to the little group of Protheros huddled cosily in a corner. Diamond was doing most of the talking, while Bonnie gazed at her wide-eyed and Ernie beamed fondly at them both.

"I'll tell you something for free," Windy went on, removing a stray piece of fag-paper from his lips, "you play a darn sight better than Joe Prince. Better tempo."

"Joe Prince? Is he the drummer that didn't show up?"

"That's right. Dead unreliable, always was. Play your cards right and Nev might take you on regular. Give Joe the boot, once and for all. Gawd knows, Di's been at him to do it for years." Prince's laugh was even wheezier than his cough.

" 'Fraid I couldn't leave Dunmold," I said, "not right now." This, apart from being the truth, was the most tactful way I could find of saying that a permanent job with the Blue City Swingers was the last thing I wanted.

"Pity." Windy must have noticed the direction in which my eyes were goggling because he added slyly, "But I can't say I blame you. She's a great-looking chick."

Most of the band talked like this, a sort of pseudo-hip patois with its roots in Hollywood, circa 1935.

I said coolly, "If you mean Bonnie Prothero, it just so happens I used to know her, but I don't think she's noticed me yet."

"Better make sure she does, then." Windy

chuckled and choked.

"Okay, boys. Time's up." Neville was doing his best to sound as if he was in command. He glanced over at his wife, who clearly had no intention of winding up her conversation till she was good and ready. With a sigh he said, "We may as well go over that instrumental again."

Windy's words rang in my ear. *Make her take notice.* Now, for a drummer, that's quite a challenge. Two bars in I switched to a higher gear. No longer content to take a back seat, metaphorically speaking, I moved into the front line, grabbing the musical initiative and leaving the rest of them floundering way behind. If Neville tried to stop me I was unaware of it, mainly because I didn't bother to look at him. I was on my own, a solo performer, a virtuoso in full flight. It was, though I say it myself, one of my more electric performances. If Bonnie Prothero hadn't noticed me by now she must be living inside a sound-proof bubble.

When I finished the silence was deafening.

Neville cleared his throat. "Very nice," he said dryly. "I'm sure we're all impressed. Now that you've got it out of your system, whatever it was, maybe we could—"

"What's that boy doing there?" Ernie had come to stand in front of the band and was glaring up at me. "He's not a musician."

Too late I realized what I'd done. In trying to make Bonnie aware of my presence I'd also alerted her father. If by now he'd read what was written in that notebook it must seem to him the way it had seemed to me earlier about the Protheros, that the world was suddenly full of Mack MacBrides.

"I must take issue with you there." Neville's tone

was cold. "He's not, I grant you, a professional but he *is* a musician – and a damn good one, at least when he remembers he's supposed to be part of an ensemble."

This was embarrassing, having Neville Brand take my part against his brother-in-law. It confused the issue. Even more confusing was the fact that Bonnie had come to stand behind Ernie and was also staring.

Ernie's eyes narrowed. "I know who he is all right. What I don't understand is why—"

Mrs Brand laid a hand on her brother's arm as if to soothe him. "Our drummer didn't turn up. Neville had to find a replacement fast and this boy happened to be around. We didn't have any choice."

He seemed a little thrown by this, as if unsure how to react, and glared at me in a way that made me seriously consider making my last Will and Testament before too much time elapsed. True, I had only my drum-kit worth bequeathing; I decided to leave it to Harry Gordon, for my successor in the band.

She pulled at his arm. "Let's go and have a drink."

Reluctantly he let himself be drawn away. Bonnie stayed where she was.

"We'd better call it a day," Neville said, defeated. "Next band-call's tomorrow afternoon, two-thirty sharp."

The band started packing up their instruments. On my way down from the podium he called me over. "Never, never do that to me again," he muttered. "I've enough problems right now without you adding to them."

Yes, and I reckoned I knew exactly what they were. Evading his eyes, I mumbled, "Sorry, sir."

"God save me from amateurs who think they're Buddy Rich," he said bitterly, and turned away.

I was still smarting from this when a breathy

female voice said, "Hi, Mack. I guess you don't remember me, but we were at—"

"Botley Road Juniors," I finished for her. "Mrs Claymore's class."

We stood, drinking each other in. She was even better in close-up. "You've changed," I said. "No freckles. And you have an American accent."

"That's because I live in the States now. Mom married a Texan."

This explained the glossiness. She had the perfect teeth of a soap-star and the golden glow of someone accustomed to lounging around outdoor swimming pools.

"It must seem strange," I said, "to be back in Dunmold."

"It's great. I haven't seen my Dad for years, or Kevin, or Bill and Georgie. They're all being so nice to me. It's wonderful to be home."

Grief, were those actually tears welling up in her big brown eyes? Was it possible for anyone to shed tears of joy at being back in the bosom of the Protheros? She made me think of a helpless kitten plonked down in a nest of vipers.

She smiled at me, reducing my bone marrow to a jelly that would prolong any dog's active life. "You're a fantastic drummer, Mack."

"Thanks." I tried to look modest. "Fact is, I don't usually play with this sort of band. Not my kind of music."

"Nor mine." She had the sort of transparent face that reflected every passing thought, and I saw at once when an idea struck her. "Are you going to disco tomorrow night, the one at Dad's place?"

"The Pink Flamingo?" I did a quick re-think. "Er, well . . . yes, as a matter of fact, I was thinking of dropping in for a while."

"Oh, that's great . . ."

"Bonnie!" Ernie Prothero's voice, bellowing from the door, broke rudely into our dialogue. "Bonnie, your aunt wants to talk to you."

"Coming, Dad." As she waltzed away she murmured, "See you, Mack."

"See you," I echoed, as feebly as a love-sick newt.

Chapter Nine

Next morning I met up with Grady at the Seagull caff. Several times I was on the point of saying casually, "You'll never guess who's back in town," but something stopped me each time. I wasn't sure I had complete control over my tone of voice. It might give me away, especially as Grady had an uncanny knack of being able to read my mind. So far our relationship had remained unclouded by either of us becoming seriously involved with a member of the opposite sex. It was true I had my occasional flings, but Grady treated all boys, apart from me, with a kind of amused contempt. Why she should regard me differently I'd no idea, but I was glad she did. She was a good mate, and, when it came to dealing with the Protheros, could be a very useful one.

I asked casually, "Fancy going to that disco tonight?"

"Not much. Why?" Her eyes narrowed. "Don't tell me you've changed your mind?"

"Could be." My tone was so laid back it was practically supine. "Better than staying at home."

"That's not what you told Jennifer Wainwright."

"Ah, well . . . no place for a kid like her."

"No place for you, either, Mack. What's got into you? You hate the Pink Flamingo." Her face cleared. "Oh, I get it. More detective work."

"Something like that." I felt a first-class toad, lying to her.

"In that case I suppose I'd better come, if only to keep an eye on you."

"Thanks." Somewhat differently I added, "Maybe you could bring your judo class along as well, just in case."

"I daresay some of them will be there anyway." She raised an eyebrow. "Expecting trouble?"

"Not especially, but you never know."

It would even up the numbers, I thought. Protheros v MacBride & O'Rourke plus a few black, brown and orange belts.

I asked Grady, "You got a soccer match this afternoon?"

She nodded. "We're playing Medbourne's Second XI. Here, at their request. I don't think they dare risk being annihilated in front of their home crowd." Her green eyes glinted with relish. There was nothing the Dunmold Women's F.C. liked better than a good scrap on the soccer pitch with an all-male team. "You got anything on, Mack?"

"Only another band practice," I said with a sigh.

Meanwhile the morning stretched before me, long and Bonnie-less. There was always the hope, of course, I might bump into her by chance. Glancing idly through the window I said, "How d'you fancy a stroll along the pier? I'd like to take a look inside the

Pavilion, seeing I've got to perform there tomorrow night. I've almost forgotten what the place looks like."

Grady left the Honda parked ouside the caff and we crossed the road to the pier. It was now open, a steady stream of bored-looking Easter visitors flowing through the turnstile to wander aimlessly up and down its crumbling length, breathing in what was left of the ozone. On a day like today, fresh and spring-like, with the tide right out and children playing on the sludge-coloured sands, nothing could be more English than Dunmold Pier. It was hard to believe it had recently been the scene of a grisly murder.

Then I saw something that made me freeze. "Grady . . . look!"

She turned. "Where?"

I pointed to the tent-like structure under the sign saying *Fortunes Told*. "Madame Olga's booth. It's open."

We both stared at the gap in the canvas. Inside, amidst the gloom, a dim light shone.

"She must have come back," Grady said.

"You think Ernie put the pressure on?"

"Maybe she wanted to come back anyway. It's a big thing in her life, this stall on the pier."

I said, "I have to speak to her."

Grady nodded. "Pretend you want your fortune told."

"But it says five quid on that notice." I turned out my pockets. "Do you think she'll accept £2.50?"

"Tell her you only want half your fortune. Preferably the good half."

"Okay." I took deep breath. "If I'm not out in twenty minutes you'd better come in after me."

"Twenty minutes is a long time," she pointed out. "You may not have that much future left, if the Protheros have anything to do with it."

"Don't remind me, even in joke." Clutching the money in my hot, sweaty palm, I approached the booth and stuck my head through the gap. "Is anyone there?"

"Just a minute." The voice was muffled, a little breathless. "All right, you can come in now."

I stepped inside. A swathe of black curtains lined the canvas, the only light came from a small table lamp with a greenish shade. At first Madame Olga was little more than a vague seated shape, but as my eyes became more used to the gloom I saw that she was wearing a veil of mauvish chiffon over her face, leaving only the eyes visible. A knotted scarf covered her head.

I cleared my throat. "Do you have special rates for students? I only have £2.50."

She took the money without quibbling. "Sit down and give me your hand."

I sat. The hand that held mine was plump and surprisingly strong. While she studied my palm I tried to think how to phrase my questions as tactfully as possible. After a moment I leaned forward to say, "We've been worried about you. Your nephew Tony—"

"Be quiet and listen," she interrupted sternly. "You are by nature inclined to be anxious. There's no need for this. Your life will take its own course, pre-destined and inescapable. I see a strong artistic streak here. You are perhaps hoping to make a career in something creative?"

"Well . . . yes, if you call catering creative. But what I really wanted to know—"

"You are also very attractive to the opposite sex. I see quite a few women in your life."

Diverted, I stared down at my hand. "Is there – would there be anyone in particular?"

Madame Olga bent closer. "There's a girl who's close to you. A pretty girl, with brown hair . . ."

This was disappointing. Not by any stretch of the imagination could you describe Bonnie's hair as "brown". "Are you sure?" I queried.

"Well, it's a very light brown, almost fair. And she has blue eyes."

She'd changed tack too swiftly, following my lead. Assuming that the girl I had in mind was fair, she'd taken a chance on her also having blue eyes. Statistically she might easily have been right, but in Bonnie's case she couldn't have been more wrong. I asked abruptly, "What about music?"

"Music?"

"Do you see any music in my hands?"

"Perhaps. But your future will almost certainly lie in catering, perhaps in the hotel business."

She was beginning to sound like a Careers Officer. What she did *NOT* sound like was Olive Pilling.

I leaned back, to get a better view of her. The general shape was right, round and dumpy, but the aura was wrong. Olive's personality was cosy and a little fey; the woman facing me gave off vibes as prickly as a thorn-bush. In short, Madame Olga was a phoney.

She seemed to sense my scepticism. "Beware of all forms of transport," she gabbled, "and take care of your health, especially your ears, nose and throat. Provided you heed my words you should have a long and happy life." She let go my hand.

I stared at her. "Is that it, then?"

"For £2.50, yes."

"It's a con," I said. "You're not Madame Olga."

She drew in a sharp breath. "Can't you read? That's what the sign says, isn't it?" Her eyes above the chiffon scarf were hard and very, very black. I felt a stirring of recognition.

"I don't care what the sign says, you're not Olive Pilling."

"Who said I was? Madame Olga's a trade name, anyone can use it."

"Not in Dunmold they can't. In Dunmold Madame Olga's always been Olive Pilling and that's who everyone expects . . ." I reached forward and tugged at the chiffon scarf before she could stop me, revealing a sallow, heavily jowled face that I'd seen before – mainly on school Open Days.

Just as I'd thought, it was the second Mrs Prothero. Ernie's gypsyish wife, imported to replace the missing Olive and allay suspicion.

Outraged, she rose to her feet. "How dare you! You wait till I tell my husband . . ."

I beat a hasty retreat.

Grady was waiting outside, leaning over the rail. "Quick," I muttered, grabbing her arm.

"Why, what –?"

"I'll tell you later."

Without stopping to see if Mrs Prothero had pursued me out of the booth, with or without her chiffon scarf, I hauled Grady down the pier and out through the turnstile.

"I thought you wanted to look inside the Pavilion," she said, as soon as our pace had slowed down.

I explained in some detail why I'd changed my mind, but leaving out the bits about the fair-haired girl and my being attractive to women, the latter

71

mainly because I was afraid Grady might laugh.

She asked, "Did Mrs Prothero recognize you, d'you think?"

"No idea. She doesn't know me all that well, so it's possible she didn't." I tried to remember what had been said. "It's true she mentioned the hotel business, but that may have been coincidence."

"What if she describes you?"

"To Ernie? I could be any one of a hundred teenagers in this town."

"Yes, but the other ninety-nine haven't shown any interest in the whereabouts of Olive Pilling. Only you." She climbed on to her waiting Honda.

"You're beginning to depress me, Grade."

"Am I?" She kicked the engine into life, then looked up at me quizzically. "Are you still sure you want to risk the Pink Flamingo tonight?"

My throat went dry. "Yeah," I croaked. "Yeah, I'm sure."

"Okay," she said with a shrug. "But I hope you know what you're doing."

Chapter Ten

The Saturday band-call was notable mainly for the foul mood Diamond Jones was in. During the practice she continually sniped at all the members of the band except me, whose presence she seemed curiously unaware of.

When Neville called a halt I was the first to leave, but Ma caught me walking through the lobby and insisted on giving me the keys to go back and lock up the banquetting room. As I reached the door I saw that Neville and Diamond were still there, arguing, so I dodged back out of sight and unashamedly listened in.

" . . . facilities are appalling," he was saying. "It's an insult to professional musicians, expecting them to appear in such a dump."

"You were the one who wanted this booking," Diamond retorted. "I only wangled it because you said that if we didn't work soon the band would fold up altogether. You know I hate this place, I always did. If we had any sense we'd cut our losses and leave before the balloon goes up."

"We can't leave now. It would damage our reputation."

"What reputation?' she demanded scornfully. "You think anyone still takes us seriously? I should have listened to Ernie all those years ago. He always said you'd never amount to anything. Marrying you was the worst career move I ever made."

"Is that so? Well. I'd like to see any other man standing by you the way I've done these ten years. You've led me one hell of a dance, Di. When I think of the times I've had to bail you out of trouble . . ."

"So what? If you wanted a quiet life you should have married someone else. At least you can't accuse me of being dull."

"You can say that again!"

Their voices were coming nearer. I took a few steps back so that it would look as if I'd only just arrived, which meant I missed the next couple of sentences. When I was within hearing range again Diamond was saying, " . . . doing all he can. I trust Ernie. He won't let us down."

Neville snorted. "I'd sooner trust a rattlesnake."

"He has our interests at heart. By the way, he's not happy about the boy."

"Well, I am. He has a tendency to show off, I grant you, but at least he has talent."

"A talent for snooping, Ernie says."

"There's no pleasing you, is there? After years of grumbling about Joe—" He broke off as we came face to face.

"Hi," I said brightly. "Ma sent me to lock up." I dangled the key in front of their noses.

For the space of about two seconds they stood as if

74

paralyzed. I could almost see their brains totting up the chances of my having overheard any of their conversation.

Diamond was the first to recover. "We were just talking about you." She switched on a smile, dazzling in its falseness. "I said to Neville, we've hardly missed our regular drummer at all, you're filling in so well."

Neville said tersely, "As long as he doesn't get starstruck again."

"Oh, he won't, I'm sure. You'll be a good boy, won't you, from now on?" She patted me on the arm with her scrawny, prehensile hand. It was as much as I could do not to shrink away. "Come along, Nev."

He followed her, meek as a slave, down the corridor.

I spent the rest of that day, on and off, trying to work out the significance of what I'd heard; but apart from balloons going up and Ernie calling me a snoop it didn't seem to amount to much. There'd been no talk, for example, of pushing old ladies off piers. Not that I'd expect it to be their main topic of conversation, but they might have referred to it, if only in passing.

Unless, of course, I was wrong about Neville having told his wife what he'd done? Maybe he was still keeping his guilty secret to himself, which would account for his habitually miserable expression. The odd thing was that I'd begun to feel almost sorry for him. Whatever I thought of his music, it was obvious that he cared about the band's future and he couldn't have had an easy life, married to a woman who, in his own words, had led him one hell of a dance. Still, he had only himself to blame, for marrying a Prothero.

But that was a train of thought I didn't care to pursue.

Entering the Pink Flamingo was like diving into a bowl of strawberry yoghurt. It was typical of Ernie that he should think along such predictable lines. Call a place Pink Something and inevitably everything inside it has to be the same sickly-sweet hue, even the lighting. The best you could say for it was that it made everyone look healthy, if rather flushed.

The music was so loud the only way you could carry on a conversation was to lip-read. I mouthed to Grady, "Do you want a drink?" and she mouthed back, "I wouldn't mind a Coke," so we went over to prop up the bar.

"How'd your match go?" I semaphored.

She showed me, thumbs up.

Tonight, I noticed, she was dressed for action in a black leather jumpsuit and high-laced trainer boots. Grady has the longest legs of anyone I know, right up to her armpits. I saw plenty of boys eyeing her over and I waited to see if any of them would ask her to dance, but nobody did. I don't think they had the courage.

"Mack, you came! I knew you would." Only Jennifer Wainwright's screech could be high-pitched enough to make itself heard above the amplifiers. "Let's dance."

I cast an agonized look at Grady, but she only raised an eyebrow and shrugged. Clearly she had no intention of coming to my rescue. Jennifer, in a short black skirt and skimpy sweater, dragged me on to the floor.

"I thought I told you not to come," I said to her sternly as she jiggled around me in what I suppose was meant to be an alluring manner.

"What?"

"I said, I TOLD YOU NOT TO COME."

"Can't hear you." Smiling, she continued to jiggle.

I gave up and took the opportunity instead to look around for Bonnie. So far there was no sign of any of the Protheros. Only Shoulders MacLean, Ernie's hefty henchman and bouncer, leaned against a door jamb, keeping a bloodshot eye on things in case of trouble. I could have told him, until the Protheros arrived there was unlikely to be any trouble.

"Hi, Mack! Come dance with me." I was literally poached, right under Jennifer's nose, by Sandra, the waitress from the Bellevue. In a frilly get-up totally unsuitable for her age, she circled around me with a predatory gleam in her eye, seeming oblivious to the fact she must be the oldest hoofer there by about twenty years. A furious Jennifer somehow managed to muscle her way back in, so that I ended up dancing with both of them at once. One fourteen-year-old partner, one over forty: it seemed I was doomed to be chased by the wrong kind of woman. Again I cast a pleading eye in Grady's direction, but she remained unmoved.

Then they arrived. Wild Bill, Kevin the kid, Gormless George Junior and Bonnie, the three boys clustered around her protectively like Doberman Pinschers guarding a Chihuahua. She saw me, I swear she saw me, but before she could so much as smile in my direction they'd whisked her over to a table and started dancing attendance on her, supplying her with drinks and crisps and peanuts and all the other little luxuries the Pink Flamingo went in for.

It was Gormless Georgie who asked her to dance.

This suited me fine. If it had been Bill or Kevin I might have thought twice about cutting in, but Georgie didn't worry me half so much. With ruthless efficiency I ditched both my partners and sashayed across the room, pretending to stumble when I reached them in order to knock Goergie out of the way, like a croquet ball, and take his place.

Bonnie's brown eyes lit up when she saw me. "Hi, Mack. It's great to see you again."

I smiled at her. "Great to see you too."

This tender exchange took place, naturally, without benefit of sound. Meaningful conversation being out of the question, we resorted from then on to eye contact. You can say a lot with eyes. Bonnie's were especially eloquent. The messages they sent made my legs feel quite rubbery, like two strips of overcooked pasta. So intent was I on reading them, and replying in kind, that I failed to notice when a space cleared around us. Hovering on the edge stood the Prothero Gang, looking ominous.

And that's putting it mildly.

They began to advance on me, solid as a brick wall. Like in a silent film, all the action seemed exaggerated and strangely slow. First Bonnie was pulled away from me and thrust out of sight, behind Wild Bill. Then Kevin took a swipe at my chin, but I ducked and he hit the person behind me, who happened to be Jennifer Wainwright. She seemed shell-shocked for a moment, and stood with one hand pressed to her face. Then she started to cry.

That did it. I went for Kevin with both fists blazing and next thing I knew the world fell in on top of me. Suddenly there were a lot more than three Protheros – there was a whole army of them, and they were all putting the boot in at once. What happened next I witnessed from floor level, where I lay clutching my stomach and writhing in agony, so all I could see was feet. Or, to be more accurate, assorted male footwear. Black Doc Martens (Wild Bill's), similar but badly scuffed (Gormless Georgie's) and brown with cuban heels (Kevin's), all weaving and shifting around me to get into a good position for the next blow.

Then, to my extreme relief, a pair of neat black trainer boots arrived on the scene. A couple of seconds later Kevin landed on the floor beside me, closely followed by Wild Bill. I was waiting for Georgie to join them when two large casuals took up a stance in front of my nose and Shoulders MacLean's voice thundered, "OUT!"

There was an eerie silence. The music had stopped.

Grady helped me up. Watched by curious eyes, we made our way to the exit. I didn't look for Bonnie, I was in no fit state. All I wanted was to leave the Pink Flamingo by the quickest possible route.

Outside, I leaned against the wall and was extremely sick.

Grady waited. When I'd recovered she demanded, "What got into you, Mack? You do realize that was Bonnie Prothero you were chatting up?"

"I wasn't chatting her up," I gasped. "We weren't even talking."

"You didn't need to," she said caustically. "I only hope for your sake her father wasn't watching."

"He wasn't there."

"Want to bet? My guess is he was upstairs in his office with his eyes glued to closed circuit television. Didn't you notice the cameras?" When I shook my head she heaved a despairing sigh. "You must be out of your mind, that's all I can say."

"My mind's okay," I said with a groan. "It's my stomach that doesn't feel so good. Mind you, it could have been worse. I suppose I should be thankful Kevin's fist didn't land on my face."

"Might have been better if it had." She climbed on

to the Honda. "You're a menace, MacBride. It's a good thing I'm immune to your fatal charm."

"Talking of Kevin's fist," I said, "I suppose I ought to check that Jennifer's okay. After all, it was my fault—"

"Leave her," Grady snapped. "Your other girl-friend – the waitress – took her off to the cloakroom. She'll sort her out." She revved the engine. "Get on, I'll take you home."

"Okay, but drive slowly. I'm feeling fragile."

She took me at my word, although I could still feel waves of disapproval wafting in my direction. We were crawling along the sea front at about 25 mph when we saw lights on the beach and a little crowd gathered halfway down the shingle.

"What's going on?" I said.

"Wait here. I'll find out." Grady left the bike propped against the kerb with me still on it and disappeared over the esplanade railings.

I began to feel sick again, and not only because of the blow to my stomach. A fearful dread was beginning to take hold of me.

Within a couple of minutes Grady returned. "They've found a body," she said shortly. "It's just been washed up by the tide."

"I knew it! Now perhaps somebody will listen." I groaned as the full implication hit me. "Poor old Olive . . ."

"Whoever it is, it isn't Olive Pilling. In fact it isn't a woman at all. It's a man!"

Chapter Eleven

Next morning at the Seagull Caff the talk was all of the drowned man. Most people thought he must have been swept off the deck of a passing trawler, although no seaman had been reported missing; and there was some pretty fanciful speculation as to his identity, ranging from Buster Crabbe to Lord Lucan.

During all this Grady and I sat apart, saying little. Though naturally relieved that the corpse had turned out not to be Olive Pilling we were both, I think, troubled by the coincidence. While it's true that drownings are not unknown in Dunmold, they tend to happen mainly in the summer months when visitors make the mistake of thinking the sea is user-friendly, which it isn't. That there should apparently have been two within a few days of each other I found frankly unbelievable.

"You're sure it was a woman's scream you heard?" asked Grady, whose thoughts were obviously running parallel to mine.

"I was at the time. Now I'm beginning to wonder."
I traced pensive patterns in the scum on my coffee
with a spoon. "Do men scream in times of stress?
Surely they'd be more inclined to yell."

"Depends how scared they are."

"If only we knew who he was," I added tentatively,
"You didn't, I suppose, get a good look at him?"

"Pretty good. But I don't think I'd have recognized
him, even if it was someone I'd known all my life. He
was blown up like a barrage balloon."

I shuddered. "Still wearing clothes?"

"What was left of them."

"Surely they'll help to identify him? There might
be a letter in his pocket. Or an address book.
Something to give the police a lead."

"After several days in the water? The ink would
run."

"A cheque card, then. They could trace him
through his account number."

"Don't forget it's Easter. No banks will be
working. It could be days till we know for sure,
probably not until the papers report on the inquest."

I sighed. "Meanwhile we still don't know what's
happened to Olive."

"Perhaps Vera was telling the truth and she really
has gone to Brighton."

"With a cut telephone wire? And Gormless
Georgie sitting outside in a parked van and Ernie's
wife taking her place on the pier?" I shook my head.
"The Protheros are at the bottom of this, you can bet
your sweet life. Whatever goes on in Dunmold,
they're always at the bottom of it."

Grady leaned back in her chair and significantly
folded her arms.

I raised the scummy coffee to my lips – and almost

choked when a voice said, "Oh Mack, I've been looking for you all over. I was so worried about you."

Talk of the devil. Except that this particular Prothero was looking deliciously angelic in a pale blue angora sweater and tight white jeans that were never bought this side of the Pond. Last night I'd vowed never to have anything to do with Bonnie Prothero again; but this morning, with her big brown eyes fixed limpidly on my face, I could feel my resolve already beginning to crack.

"Jennifer told me where I'd find you," she added.

Until she said that I hadn't even noticed the small, brooding figure behind her. Jennifer Wainwright, sporting one purplish eye and attended by her side-kick Noella Spink, glowered at me with all the venom of Medusa hell-bent on revenge.

"Hi," I said cautiously, addressing all three of them. I felt reluctant to commit myself further without knowing exactly how they were disposed towards me although in Jennifer's case it wasn't hard to guess.

"I feel terrible, Mack." Bonnie slid onto a vacant chair. She cast a quick, uncertain glance at Grady's impassive face before directing the full beam of her gaze back to me. "I'd no idea the boys would behave like that. I don't know what came over them. I guess they didn't realize we knew each other before."

I cleared my throat, hoping it would pass for a comment. For the life of me I couldn't think of anything adequate to say.

Bonnie stretched out one tanned, pink-nailed hand to stroke my cheek. "Your poor face."

"*His* poor face!" Jennifer snorted. "There's not a mark on it. How about my eye?"

I cleared my throat again. "Yeah, I'm sorry about

that. I didn't know you were standing so close, otherwise I wouldn't have ducked."

"Yes, you would," said Grady. Her expression was still impassive, but there was a definite gleam in her eye. "Your reactions have always been quick, MacBride, when it comes to getting out of trouble."

I began to feel like the beleaguered male. Three against one, with only Bonnie manifestly on my side. Grady seemed to have decided, for reasons best known to herself, to sit on the fence and spectate.

"Here . . ." I fumbled in my pockets for a coin and pressed it into Jennifer's hand. "Why don't you buy yourself an ice-cream. Have it on me. I know it won't make up for what happened, but it might make you feel better."

She stared down at the coin. "One ice-cream isn't much. How about a Knickerbocker Glory?" She glanced at Noella. "Each."

"Okay." Resignedly I fumbled for another coin. "As long as you eat them at another table. I'm trying to have a private conversation here."

Jennifer pouted rebelliously but she went, Noella in tow.

Bonnie put her hand on my arm. "That was real nice of you, Mack."

Grady pushed back her chair and stood up.

"You don't have to go as well," I said hastily.

"Yes, I do. I have to see a man about a corpse."

"What man?"

"Reporter I know on the *Dunmold Recorder*. That way we'll be sure of hearing the news as soon as it breaks." Her gaze flickered briefly over Bonnie and back to me. "Cheers, Mack."

"Cheers." I turned to find Bonnie gazing after Grady's departing figure.

"That girl kinda scares me," she confessed. "She scares Georgie too. I know because he told me. And what did she mean about a corpse?"

"Private joke," I said. "Bonnie, I'm going to be honest with you. Your family don't like me any more than they like Grady. What's more, it's mutual."

"I know," she said calmly. "Pa told me I wasn't to see you again. But I told him, heck, that wasn't the way I'd been brought up. Mom let me choose my own friends. She never plays the heavy parent."

My estimation of Bonnie went up several notches. So she wasn't just a pretty face. Anyone who dared stand up to Ernie Prothero, daughter or no daughter, had to have guts.

"What did he say?" I asked curiously.

"Oh, he was mad at me at first. But then Aunt Diamond took him aside and talked to him. I didn't hear what she said but it sure made him change his mind. When he came back he said I could go ahead and see you as much as I liked."

This made me uneasy. Why should Diamond, who always gave the impression she disliked me intensely, plead my case? And why had Ernie given in so quickly? The only explanation I could think of was that they wanted to keep tabs on me. Somehow they'd persuade Bonnie to give a blow-by-blow account of our conversations every time she returned to the family fold. One way and another, our relationship seemed fraught with danger.

I glanced through the window of the caff, half-expecting to see the Prothero Gang lurking outside. But there was no one there, not even a parked white van.

Bonnie said, "Well?"

"Well?" I echoed uncomprehendingly.

"Aren't you going to ask me for a date?"

"What? Oh. Yeah. Trouble is, tonight I have to play with the Blue City Swingers."

"Yes, I know. I'm coming to hear you." Her gaze was still fixed expectantly on my face.

"And this afternoon I have to work. I promised my father—"

"Mack, don't you want to see me again?"

"Of course I do, but—"

"We don't have much time. On Tuesday I have to leave for London, to meet up with Mom. We fly home Friday." Her eyes were suspiciously moist. "It may be months before I get back to England again."

My sense of self-preservation flew out of the window. "Oh, what the heck!" I said recklessly. "Okay, let's meet this afternoon."

The sun came out in her smile. "Where?"

"Pier entrance, four o'clock. We can decide then what we're going to do." Uncomfortably aware that Jennifer Wainwright, halfway through her Knicker-bocker Glory, was monitoring our every move, I clambered to my feet. "Got to get back to the hotel. Sunday lunch. Always a bit of a rush."

Bonnie glanced at her watch. "I'd better go too. We're having a real family party today. Old English beef and Yorkshire pudding."

It was reassuring to know the Protheros could do anything so conventional as sit round a table and eat a Sunday joint. Although I wouldn't mind betting it had fallen off the back of somebody's lorry, probably the Wainwrights'.

We parted outside the caff and she went off up the High Street, swinging along with her easy trans-atlantic stride. There was still no sign of a white van, so why did I have the feeling that I was being watched

– and not only by Jennifer's black eye?

When I reached the Bellevue I found a police car parked outside.

"Trouble?" I asked Ma, who was behind the reception desk.

"Just a little enquiry, something they wanted to ask Mr Brand." She busied herself with moving keys around on hooks, but I could tell she was nervous. This suggested she knew more than she was giving away.

"Mr Brand? Why, what's he done?" (As if I didn't know.)

"Nothing, poor man. He's just . . . helping the police with their enquiries."

Now this, as any streetwise citizen knows, is media jargon for being guilty as hell. I persisted, "Does it have anything to do with the guy who was drowned?"

Ma looked up sharply. "What do you know about that?"

"Grady and I saw him last night, just after they fished him out of the water." A slight bending of the truth: I'd been in no fit state to look at a bloated corpse. "Have they found out who he is – er, was?"

She said grudgingly, "It seems they have their suspicions."

So they must have found some form of identification. Something, moreover, that led them straight to Neville Brand.

Even as I drew breath to press her further the lift door opened and out stepped Diamond Jones with two police officers and a very sick-looking Neville. He didn't so much as glance in our direction but walked straight past the desk towards the revolving door.

Diamond, however, hung back. She said to one of the policemen, "You don't need me, do you?"

"No, madam." He sounded solicitous, sympathetic. "There's no point in you coming as well."

"Right." She raised her voice. "Neville, I'll see you later."

He gave no sign that he'd heard her but carried on pushing his way through the door, followed by the two policemen.

Diamond turned to Ma and me, who were both gawping like morons. She seemed to be calculating whether or not to satisfy our blatant curiosity. "Shocking thing," she remarked. "Seems that one of our band has been drowned. They found a medallion on his body with the name Blue City Swingers. Neville's gone to the mortuary to identify him."

One of the band? I could think only of Windy, with his sad bloodhound eyes and wheezy cough.

"Oh dear," murmured Ma. "I'm so sorry to hear that. Which – er, one—?"

"Joe Prince." Diamond's gaze rested on me briefly, hard as her name. "The drummer your son replaced. Well, I'd better be on my way. You know we're not in to lunch, don't you? My brother invited us over to his house. I expect Neville will come on later, after he's finished at the mortuary."

For once even Ma seemed lost for words. We watched in silence as Diamond Jones, apparently unmoved by the tragic demise of a Blue City Swinger, sauntered across the lobby and out of the hotel.

Chapter Twelve

Dead men's shoes.

That's all I could think about in the kitchen while making gravy for the Roast Norfolk Turkey, our Easter Sunday Special – how I'd taken Joe Prince's place with the Blue City Swingers. Before I'd been only an onlooker, an objective amateur sleuth; now I felt involved up to my neck, and oddly guilty. I should have said something earlier, done something. Now it was too late.

It must have been Joe who was pushed off the pier, I felt certain of it. The connection with Neville Brand couldn't be mere coincidence. But what had he been doing in Dunmold three days before the rest of the band arrived?

"Nigel!" Dad groaned at me. "Have a care, for pity's sake. That gravy's got lumps in it the size of ping-pong balls."

"Okay, I'll use the strainer."

Sandra stuck her head through the hatch. "Hitler

just came in. He asked me to give you a message."

"Neville Brand?" I lowered my voice. "What's he doing back here? He's supposed to be lunching at the Protheros."

"Said he didn't feel hungry. Well, no more would I after a trip to the mortuary."

"You know about that?"

"News travels." She flapped her lashes at me, "Don't you want to know the message?"

"Yeah, okay, what is it?"

"He said to tell you there's a band call at three at the Pavilion. Oh, and be sure to have your drum kit ready in the lobby by 2.30. The van's coming to pick up the stuff and take it over there."

"Okay. But the band call's out of the question. I've – er, made other arrangements."

"You can tell him that yourself, Treasure." She pinched my cheek, a little too hard for auntly affection. "I warn you, he's in a funny mood."

She was right about the mood. While the band and I loaded our gear into the van Neville danced around like a cat on hot bricks, edgily overseeing every move but doing little himself. His face was sickly pale, his moustache even blacker by contrast. He said nothing about his trip to the mortuary and I hadn't the courage to ask what happened. Nor, it seemed, had anyone else. The rest of the band were morose and mainly silent, clearly shattered by the death of their erstwhile drummer.

When we'd finished Neville said, "You'd better come along, MacBride, to unload your kit the other end. My brother-in-law's fixed it for us to drive right on to the pier."

I didn't argue. The pier was where I'd arranged to meet Bonnie anyway.

There was a stiff breeze blowing off the sea, whipping the awnings into a frenzy. It rocked the van as we drove along the most exposed part of the pier and I distinctly heard a couple of boards crack under our wheels. The wisdom of driving anything heavy on to such a tacky edifice seemed to me decidedly dubious, but presumably Ernie didn't give a hang if his brother-in-law, plus a load of musicians, landed in the drink.

At the Pavilion we unloaded our gear and set up the stage. It was some time since I'd last set foot inside the building and I was shocked to see how far it had been allowed to deteriorate: plaster peeling off the walls, shabby paint-work, threadbare upholstery on the tip-up seats. Tonight, of course low-key lighting would fool the public into thinking they were at a smart venue. That's if anyone came.

Neville, still jumpy, fussed around the lighting console. Windy sat down on the stage and lit up a fag. I crouched on my hunkers beside him and asked, keeping my voice low, "Did you hear about Joe Prince?"

He nodded. "Poor old Joe. Mind you, it don't surprise me. He'd pretty well come to the end of things, I reckon. Maybe this was the only way out."

"You think he committed suicide?"

"Looks like it. Lord knows he had troubles enough."

"What sort of troubles?"

"Money, mostly. He couldn't kick the gambling habit." Windy shook his head sadly. "And he was going deaf, which meant he was near the end of his life as a musician."

"So why did Neville keep him on?"

"Search me. Old times' sake, I suppose."

This made Neville sound like a great big softie, which in the circumstances I found hard to believe. On the other hand, bad musicianship hardly seemed a sufficient motive for murder. Surely it would have been easier just to give him the sack?

Unless, of course, Joe had had some sort of a hold over Neville. Maybe he knew something Neville wanted to keep quiet. Blackmail – now that would be an excellent reason for pushing someone off a pier.

"Windy," I said, "did Joe have a very high-pitched voice?"

He stared at me. "Why d'you ask that?"

"I'm trying to get some kind of a picture of him. After all, I am taking his place. It's only natural I should be curious."

He seemed to accept this as reasonable. "No, as a matter of fact his voice was as rough as a ton of gravel. You couldn't call it high-pitched, not by any stretch of the imagination. He was an odd-looking guy, bald as a coot, bit on the fat side."

Must have made quite a splash.

A thought struck me. What if the splash and the scream hadn't come from the same person? A man fell off the pier, a woman screamed . . .

"Poor old Joe," Windy added morosely. "He couldn't even swim."

By this time the rest of the band were arriving and somehow a sort of rehearsal had started up before I could make my excuses. Keeping strict time with my left hand on the side drum, I glanced at the watch on my right wrist. Three-thirty and I was due to meet Bonnie at four. Oh well, it wouldn't hurt me to put in half-an-hour's practise. At least it meant I could keep an eye on Neville.

He foxed me completely. That any musician could

be so apparently lacking in emotion seemed a contradiction in terms. There was no enjoyment in the way he worked. On the contrary, his insistence on a rigidly strict tempo – and his irritation if any of us deviated by so much as a micro-beat – suggested a kind of pent-up desperation. I didn't fancy telling him I wanted to leave early.

It had gone four and I was still trying to work up the courage when suddenly Diamond Jones appeared and Neville stopped immediately. "Sorry I'm late, boys," she said. "I got talking, you know how it is." Her gaze slid past her husband to me. "You'd better go now. Bonnie's waiting for you."

"What?" Neville looked scandalized. "We're in the middle of a rehearsal, in case you hadn't noticed."

"We can manage. Let the boy go, he has a date with my niece." She jerked her head at me, as if urging me to leave quickly, while I had the chance.

I took it.

The wind outside nearly took my breath away. I found Bonnie sheltering in the amusement arcade, hugging her arms inside a pastel blue zipper jacket. "I'd forgotten how cold it can be in England," she said. "Can we go somewhere warm?"

The only warm place I could think of was the Rialto Cinema. Studio One was showing a film I'd never heard of, something about a woman and a window, and as the first showing wasn't over yet I suggested we wait in the foyer for ten minutes rather than spoil our enjoyment by seeing the end.

The real reason was that I wanted a chance to question her. Tab-keeping could be made to work both ways.

"How was your family party?" I asked, propping myself up against the wall.

"Okay." Bonnie frowned. "Except I don't think I understand my Aunt Diamond."

"Why, what did she say?"

"Oh, it's not what she says exactly, more the way she acts, like she gets a real kick out of being mean to people. You should hear the way she talked to my stepmother. I'm not exactly crazy about my stepmother myself, but she was trying real hard to be nice to Aunt Diamond and Aunt Diamond kept making snide remarks about her behind her back."

I could imagine the scene, the brittle blonde woman and the dark heavy one, a clash of temperamental opposites.

"The Protheros," I said, for the moment forgetting that Bonnie was a member of the clan, "don't like outsiders."

She gave me an unhappy look. "They don't like you either, Mack. Dad called you a snoop. But when I asked him why he wouldn't tell me."

"He didn't stop you seeing me, though?"

"No," she said doubtfully. "But I don't think he's too happy about it."

I'd already guessed that. Ever since we left the pier a thin, slouched figure had been shadowing us. Kevin must be aware by now, I thought with some satisfaction, that he was in for a long, boring wait.

The doors opened and a trickle of people came out. Bonnie and I went in to take our seats, not in the back row – that would have been too much of a cliché – but in the middle stalls, surrounded by empty space. This meant we could go on talking without risk of being overheard.

I rested my arm casually along the back of her seat. "Did your aunt tell you where her husband went?"

"She said he'd gone to visit an old friend. But I

don't think that was true. I think he just didn't want to come to lunch."

"Your family doesn't seem to think too highly of Neville Brand," I said, idly winding one of her blonde curls round my finger. "Do you know why?"

"Only that Dad says he's a loser and Aunt Diamond did the wrong thing by marrying him just because he had his own band and she thought it would help her singing career. Dad can't think why she's stuck with him all these years."

I found this puzzling myself. Maybe, I thought, Diamond cared more for her husband than was immediately obvious. Although in some ways an ill-matched pair, they seemed to have a kind of mutual dependence. He needed her for her pzazz, she needed him for his stability.

On the other hand, it might be more complicated than that. A shared secret, perhaps: something dating back from their murky past?

"Still, it's nice to be part of the family again," Bonnie was saying. "That's what I miss most in the States, not having them all around me. They're a great bunch of people, so warm and loyal."

Could this be the Protheros she was talking about? It was hard to believe she could be so unaware of what her beloved family was really like. I stole a quick glance at her honest, straight-nosed profile and decided no, she meant every word.

The lights dimmed. Glancing over my shoulder I saw a hunched figure sitting alone three rows behind us and grinned to myself. I tightened my arm around Bonnie and she snuggled closer.

The film was pretty gory, not my style at all. It was about this woman who saw a guy being stabbed in an alleyway with more blood spurting around than you'd see in a slaughterhouse, and was now fearful for her life because the murderer heard her scream and spotted her running away. I kept my eyes closed through the worst bits, while at the same time pretending to comfort a deliciously shuddering Bonnie.

Then, suddenly, I opened them again.

A woman who witnessed a murder . . . and who was now in extreme danger because someone heard her scream.

I shot to my feet.

"Mack, where are you going?"

"Sorry, I just remembered something. Look, there's Kevin over there. You'd better go and join him."

"But Ma-ack . . ."

Her voice, following me as I made for the exit, sounded uncannily like Jennifer Wainwright's.

Chapter Thirteen

It was almost dusk when I reached Wisteria Close. As I turned the corner I heard a sharp "Pssst!" and swung round to see Grady beckoning to me. Her Honda was thrust out of sight behind a privet hedge. "Don't go any further," she warned. "Ernie's lying in wait and I think he's getting ready to pounce."

I stared at her in amazement. "How long have you been here?"

"About half-an-hour. I came straight from the *Recorder* office. Remember that reporter I told you about? He was at the mortuary when Neville Brand came to identify the body."

"So you know it was Joe Prince?"

She nodded. It occurred to me Neville must have been in quite a dilemma, not knowing whether to identify the body positively or not; but if he hadn't somebody else might have done and that would only have made things worse.

I asked Grady, "What brought you to Wisteria Close?"

"Just a hunch. Olive must be involved somehow or Ernie wouldn't be so interested in her. And if she wasn't the victim then she must have been a witness. It's the only explanation."

"Just what I've been thinking." I didn't add that my own thought processes had had a little help from the Rialto Cinema, Studio One. "I reckon she's been holed up inside that bungalow all the time. It must have been her I heard moving about when I was talking to Vera."

Grady nodded. "As Ernie knew very well. That's why he had the boys keeping watch."

"He'd probably also been badgering her on the phone, which would explain why she cut the wire." I cast another wary look along the road. "We have to move her out of there to somewhere safe. The question is how?"

"There's an alleyway running behind the bungalows with gates into their back gardens. I already looked."

"Great! How do we get to it?"

"Down here." She pointed to a path running parallel with the first front garden. "Come on, I'll show you."

I followed her. After a short distance the path took a sharp turn to the right, between allotments on one side and the rear of the bungalows on the other. "Which one is the Pillings'?"

"Number's on the gate."

I glanced at the back of No 8. There was no sign of anyone looking out; but then both sisters were probably glued to the front, watching Ernie.

Cautiously Grady opened the gate. The hinges

creaked slightly, not loud enough to draw attention. We walked up to the back door, but as Grady was about to knock I pulled her to one side. "If Vera answers you know she'll only clam up. It's Olive we want. I'm going to try to get through a window."

"There's a ventilator open. Looks like the bathroom." Grady eyed it dubiously. "It's narrow, though."

"I'm pretty thin. Give me a leg up, will you?"

Grady, whipcord strong, gave me a boost that shot me halfway up the wall. I grabbed the drainpipe and felt around for a toe-hold. Then, with one foot on the window-sill, I measured myself against the open ventilator. Grady was right, it was far too narrow, even for a skinny bloke like me. I stuck my arm through instead and felt around for the window catch.

Somebody smacked my hand. A shaky female voice said. "Go away. I won't say anything, I promise. Just leave us alone."

I withdrew my hand hastily and peered through the gap. It was Olive all right, her face rounder than her sister's, her pale blue eyes bulging with fright. "It's all right, Miss Pilling, it's only me – Mack, from the hotel. I've come to help you . . ."

"Who?"

"Nigel MacBride. I'm a friend of Tony's. Don't you recognize me?" I tried to show as much of my face as possible, which wasn't easy while balancing on the narrow ledge. "Look, you must have seen me loads of times. When I was a kid you gave me peppermints . . ."

"Nigel, is it really you? I thought it was that awful Prothero man."

"He's still round at the front, though probably not

99

for much longer. Could you please let me in?"

She looked apprehensive. "Well, I'm not sure . . ."

"I'm on your side, I promise you. I don't like Ernie Prothero any more than you do."

This seemed to convince her. She had a slight struggle with the catch before the window flew outward so abruptly it nearly knocked me off the ledge.

"Thanks." I sat astride the sill with one foot in the wash basin. "Listen, we don't have much time. We've got to get you away from here before Ernie forces an entry."

She clutched at the chiffon scarf around her throat. "He can't get into the bathroom. I've locked the door."

"That won't stop him. You're in danger, Miss Pilling."

"Yes, I know." Her bottom lip wobbled. "But I don't know what to do."

"I think you have to go to the police. You saw something, didn't you, that night on the pier? You saw a man pushed into the sea . . ."

She nodded, her double chin quivering.

"And then you screamed —"

"No, no, it wasn't me that screamed. It was her."

"Her?"

"The woman he was trying to strangle. She screamed and then another man came running out of the Pavilion, but by then it was too late. She'd pushed him over."

"*She* pushed him over?"

"The first man, the one who was trying to strangle her. And then she ran away. She ran right past me, down the pier. I should have stopped her, but I was too afraid."

Poor old Olive, she must have been living in fear for days. I said, "But she saw you – and knew that you'd recognized her?"

She nodded, pressing both hands to her lips. "I knew her from the old days. Please, don't ask me to tell you who she was."

There was no need. Mentally I was busy re-writing the scenario of that fatal night. So Diamond had also been on the pier – but how had I missed her? It could only have happened when I went down to the beach and was staring out to sea. During those few short minutes she must have sprinted along the esplanade, back to the hotel, and bumped into Jennifer Wainwright on the way. Hence the perfume.

But Jennifer had thought it was a man . . .

Yes, but I could have put that idea into her head myself, when I asked if he had a moustache. I remembered seeing Diamond Jones coming out of the Powder Room, wearing white cotton pants, her face like a mask. And then she had gone to join her husband in the cocktail lounge . . .

"What about the other man?" I asked Vera. "The one who came out of the Pavilion. Did he run after her?"

"Not straight away. First he went to the rail – you know, where the first man had . . ." Her voice shook and she dabbed her eyes with her scarf. "He seemed to be thinking about jumping in after him, but I don't think he had the courage. Then he turned and started to run. But when he saw me he stopped again."

"He spoke to you?"

"No, I ran off. I knew it was cowardly of me, but you see I was so terribly frightened. And then I – oh, dear!" The eye-dabbing grew fast and furious. "I hid inside my booth. It was foggy, you see, also I knew he

101

wouldn't find me. Then I heard his footsteps going away . . ."

The doorbell rang. Ignoring it, I asked, "What did you do then?"

"I stayed where I was until morning, when the workmen came to put up the sign."

That would account for her not coming home that night and Vera being worried. "But why didn't you go to the police?"

"I was too frightened. You see . . ." She swallowed hard. "I met him. Mr Prothero, I mean. He was going on to the pier that morning as I was coming off. And I was afraid he might know about me being there when his sister did You Know What. So I came straight home."

It was, though Olive didn't realize it, an admission that the woman she'd seen was Diamond Jones. At that stage, of course, Diamond hadn't told Ernie, but it could have been only a short time afterwards that I'd followed her on to the pier, where she met him outside the Pavilion.

"And he's been hounding you ever since?" I said.

"Yes! Vera told him I'd gone away but he kept telephoning and saying he wanted to see me."

"So you cut the wire?"

"We had to." She looked guilty. "I know it was wrong of us, but he was driving us out of our minds."

The door bell rang again, followed by a loud knocking and Ernie's muffled voice; then Vera's, high and querulous.

"We've got to get you out of here," I said. "Do you think you could climb through that window?"

Olive looked doubtfully down at her wine-coloured mail-order type dress for the larger woman. "I could try . . ."

"Good." I heaved myself over the wash basin to stand beside her. "I'll give you a hand. You'd better stand on the loo-seat."

She hopped up and teetered on the top, clutching my hand.

I added encouragingly, "Grady's outside. You remember Grady O'Rourke?"

Gingerly Olive advanced one knee on to the window-sill. "You mean that pretty, dark girl?"

"Yes, she is pretty dark. Ever ridden on a motor-bike?"

"Frequently." She sounded quite offended. "Used to have one myself. A 350cc flat twin Douglas."

"You're full of surprises, Miss Pilling."

By now her ample rear was blocking out the light; the rest of her was already outside, being assisted by Grady.

A crash came from the hall and suddenly Ernie's voice was much louder. "Okay, no more games. I want to see your sister."

"I keep telling you, she's not here." Vera sounded defiant but scared.

"And I know she is!"

Doors were opening and closing. He was carrying out a search.

Miraculously Olive disappeared from the window space. I stuck my head through to find out what was happening and saw Grady reeling under the unexpected weight. "Get her away," I hissed. "Take her to the police."

Behind me the door handle rattled.

"Olive?" came Ernie's voice. "I know you're in there. Come on out."

I was on the point of climbing out of the window when I hesitated. What Grady needed was time . . .

"What are you afraid of? I only want to talk to you."

Pull the other one, I thought. Tensely I waited for the sound of Grady's motor-bike, but nothing came. Give them time, more time . . .

"Olive, are you still there?"

I went closer to the door and raised my voice a couple of octaves. "Go away, you nasty man."

"Olive?"

"I don't want anything to do with you. Leave me alone."

There was a momentary silence outside the door. Then Vera's voice enquired, "Olive, are you all right?"

"No, I'm not!" I squeaked indignantly. "I'm feeling very peculiar."

"You certainly don't sound yourself—"

Ernie interrupted, "Listen, you got the wrong end of the stick, you silly old bat. We need you. We need you as a witness. You saw what happened on the pier. You know my sister's innocent. You got to stand up in court and tell them, Olive. Tell them it was self-defence."

I was silent, thinking. Could it be a bluff? But according to Olive's account what Ernie said was true; Diamond had simply been defending herself against a man who was attempting to kill her. It could just as easily have been her that went over the rail, not Joe Prince. Given Olive's testimony, no jury would find Diamond guilty of murder.

Into the silence came the roar of Grady's motor-bike, departing for the police station.

I unlocked the bathroom door.

Chapter Fourteen

"In that case," I told a startled-looking Ernie, "you'll be glad to know that Olive's on her way to the police station right now."

His eyes narrowed as he looked past me to the open window, then back at my face. "What the hell are you doing here, MacBride? You're supposed to be down the town with my daughter."

"Oh yes, you were so keen to get me out of the way you even used Bonnie—"

His hand reached out and grabbed my shirt. "What have done with her?"

"Nothing. She's with Kevin."

He dragged me closer. "You're asking for trouble, boy. I've just about had enough of you nosing around, d'you know that?"

I said hoarsely, "You'd better listen, Mr Prothero, Olive told me what she saw on the pier. And you were right, your sister could have been acting in self-defence . . ."

"What d'you mean, *could* have been? Her life was threatened, how else d'you expect her to react? It was either her or that deaf old has-been of a drummer her husband was too weak to get rid of. She didn't have any choice." He relaxed his hold a little. "That's what we gotta make people understand."

I could see now why Olive had been so important to them. Before the body was found they might have thought they could get away with it, if it hadn't been for Olive seeing the whole thing.

And now the body *was* found, and the police were asking awkward questions; Olive was the only person who could prove that Diamond was innocent. But was she really as innocent as Ernie wanted to believe? I couldn't help wondering what she'd said to Joe Prince that drove him to the point where he wanted to strangle her?

Vera stuck her head round the door, clutching the ginger tom to her bosom. "Where's my sister? What have you done with her? You haven't . . ." She peered fearfully into the empty bath.

"Don't worry, Miss Pilling, she's in safe hands." I finally managed to free myself from Ernie's hold. "Any minute now she should be at the police station."

I saw Ernie wince at the word "police" and wondered if he'd been bluffing after all. On the other hand it could be merely an automatic reflex: the Protheros' relationship with the local fuzz had never been exactly cosy.

Suddenly the light behind me darkened as two shadows appeared on the frosted glass. Wild Bill's head appeared first round the window-frame, then Gormless George's.

"Hello, Uncle. What's going on?"

"Where's the old girl? Isn't she here?"

"You're too late, you jackasses!" Ernie roared at them. "If you'd got round the back quicker, like I said, you might have been some use."

"Sorry, we couldn't find the path."

He gave an exasperated groan. "We'd better get down to the Pavilion, put Diamond in the picture. Poor girl must be going out of her mind." He added grimly, "You too, MacBride."

"I was coming anyway," I said. "You forget I've got a show to do tonight."

"Maybe. Maybe not." He stalked past Vera without a word of apology for disrupting her life for the past three days. I followed, giving the ginger tom's jaws a wide berth while muttering out of the corner of my mouth, "It's okay, Miss Pilling, the worst is over now. Nothing more can possibly happen."

Which just goes to prove I'd be no use as a fortune-teller.

We piled into the Mercedes, me in the passenger seat beside Ernie, Wild Bill and Gormless George in the back. To say I felt outnumbered would be an understatement; but for the moment, at any rate, I knew I was comparatively safe. Ernie was only bothered about reaching the pier before the police; and with their uncle around Bill and Georgie weren't so likely to act on their own vicious initiative.

At the pier entrance we disgorged and, at a word from Ernie, were admitted through the turnstile without paying. By now there was a Force Nine gale blowing and the sea was hurling itself against the stanchions below us. As we battled against the wind on our way to the Pavilion I thought, even if we have a show there won't be an audience. No one in their right senses would venture out in this weather.

Inside the Pavilion a small cocoon of light was centred on the stage; everywhere else was dark. The band was all present, apart from me, but no one was playing. As we marched towards them, Ernie in the lead, I saw Diamond and Neville, already dressed for the performance, standing apart from the rest. Diamond, in a shimmering pink dress slit up to the thigh, smoked a cigarette in quick, urgent puffs. The minute we emerged from the darkness into the pool of light she swung round to address Ernie. "What's happening? Did you get her?"

"Don't worry, Di." He climbed the steps to the stage and put a comforting arm around her shoulders. "It's going to be all right."

Diamond held back, glaring at him. "What do you mean, it's going to be all right? Did you *get* her?" Her eyes dilated. "Something's gone wrong, I know it has."

"Nothing's gone wrong," Ernie assured her. "But we need to talk a little. In private."

Neville sighed and said to the band, "Okay, boys, relax. But don't go too far away. The show's due to start in fifteen minutes."

This came as something of a shock. I glanced at my watch and saw that it was gone seven-thirty. I should have realized, it had been almost dark by the time I arrived at the Pilling bungalow. Now it was pitch-black outside, with the wind howling like a demon.

The band ambled off. Windy gave me a reassuring wink and lit up a fag. Neville shaded his eyes with his hand and peered down at Bill, Georgie and me. "Is that my drummer I see before me? Wonders will never cease, I'd almost given up hope."

Ernie jerked his head at the boys. "Bring him up here."

When they attempted to manhandle me on to the stage I shook them off. "Do you mind? This is a professional performance I'm about to give. You could at least show a little respect."

Wild Bill guffawed. Ignoring him I stepped on to the stage and said to Neville, "Sorry I'm late, but I was unavoidably delayed —"

"For pity's sake!" snorted Diamond. "Will somebody kindly tell me what's going on?"

"Over here." Ernie led her into the wings. "You too, MacBride."

"What's he got to do with it?"

"Far too much. He's the only one of us who actually got to talk to the old bird." He pulled me forward. "Go on, tell her."

"Er, well . . ." I began. "She – er, said she saw everything that happened. That is, she saw Joe Prince try to strangle you, and then you – er, pushed him over."

"There you are!" Ernie said triumphantly. "Self-defence. That means you're in the clear."

"What d'you mean, I'm in the clear?" Diamond looked from one to the other of us, her eyes like chips of blue glass. "Where's Olive Pilling *now*, that's what I want to know?"

Ernie seemed reluctant to answer, so I told her, "At the Police station."

"WHAT?"

"Any statement she makes," he said hastily, "will be along the lines of what she said to the boy. So you've no need to worry. You'll get a fair trial."

"With my record? You must be joking!" She turned on Neville, who'd been skulking behind her.

"It's all your fault. This would never have happened if you'd paid Joe off years ago, when he first started being a nuisance. You're too soft, Neville. You always leave it to me to do the dirty work."

"How could it be my fault?" Neville looked as sickly as when the police came to haul him off to the mortuary. "I didn't even know he was there, did I? I was inside this building, wondering how the heck we'd ever fetched up in such a crummy joint. It wasn't until I heard you screaming and dashed out to see what was going on that I even knew Joe was in town. If you'd told me earlier you'd seen him hanging around—"

"I was trying to protect you, wasn't I? I knew if he got to you first you'd give him everything he wanted – pay off his gambling debts *and* let him keep his job. I told him straight, his days with the band were numbered. A deaf drummer's nothing but a liability."

Neville looked sicker still. "No wonder he tried to strangle you. Joe had his professional pride, you know."

"Pride!" Diamond echoed with contempt. "He didn't know the meaning of the word. He was dragging us down, Neville. Even the kid plays better than he did." She added resentfully, "Somebody had to do something sometime, or he'd have gone on bleeding us dry for ever."

This was fascinating stuff. So I was right about the blackmail. But what did Diamond mean about her record? Presumably we weren't talking here about the Top Twenty? No, something must have happened in her past she wanted to keep quiet – something Joe Prince knew about and had used as a means of keeping his job with the band.

She appealed to her brother. "Ernie, you've got to get me out of this."

" 'Course I will, Di. I'll get you the best legal advice that money can buy—"

"That's not what I mean. I'm not going to court. I've been there already and look what happened. I mean I'm leaving."

"You can't," Neville said. "Not now. We've got a show to do."

"What show? You think anyone'll come and listen to us on a night like this? You must be out of your mind."

"Hello, Dad." Kevin's voice spoke out of the darkness. "What's the police doing here?"

We all turned to stare at the pair climbing on to the stage. To my embarrassment I saw that Bonnie was looking not only chilled and windswept but also slightly damp around the eyes. She stared back at me reproachfully.

"Police?" Ernie twitched aside the curtain. "Where?"

"Down the other end of the pier. We saw them as we came on. Somebody been fiddling the machines again?"

"Yes," said Ernie. "Yes, that's probably it. Nothing to worry about." He glanced at Bonnie. "You okay, baby?"

"Yes, Dad." But her eyes continued to pour reproach over me like a tidal wave.

Diamond ground her fag-end underfoot. "That settles it. I'm getting out."

"Don't be a fool," Ernie snapped; then more kindly, "Trust me, Di. I'm well known in this town. If anyone can get you off this hook, it's me."

This sounded to me the least convincing argument

I'd ever heard. Even Diamond looked sceptical, but she said, "Okay, turn up the house lights. Let's see how many we've got."

Neville did as she ordered. To my amazement we had an audience of three, which was three more than I'd expected. One of them was Ma, so I reckoned she and Dad must have tossed for who should come along to support me and she lost. Add to that the five spare Protheros at present on stage and it made a grand total of eight, not bad going for Dunmold on a stormy night.

"Right, let's start," said Diamond.

Neville snapped, "It's not time yet."

"Why wait around? We shan't get more punters than this." She called the rest of the band to heel, me included, and pushed us on to the stage. Luckily I'd made myself look fairly presentable for my date with Bonnie.

A sporadic, uncertain clapping greeted our appearance. Neville reluctantly followed, to no noticeable increase of applause. I took my place behind the drum kit, but as the Blue City Swingers swung into their first number I kept a wary eye on Diamond, waiting alone in the wings. She was up to something, I was sure of it. The rest of the Protheros had joined the audience, whose number had now swelled to eleven. Two men, easily identifiable as plain-clothed policemen, had already slipped into seats halfway down the auditorium.

The eleventh was Grady.

I spotted her as soon as she came in. She took a seat on the side, near the front, and gave me a brief nod. Her arrival helped to take my mind off Bonnie, whose plaintive brown orbs, radiating at me from the front row, seemed to be sapping my musical strength. If only I hadn't met her just now, I told myself, things might have been different.

And if only she weren't a Prothero.

But her family were all there, ranged on either side of her, staring fixedly at the stage. Their combined presence inhibited me, reducing my performance to something less than mediocre. I was only glad that Harry Gordon hadn't turned up to witness it.

Then it was Diamond's first solo spot. The two policemen sat up straighter in their seats. During her corncrake rendition of "My Way" and "Hey, Big Spender" she glared round furiously a couple of times at the intrusion of some extraneous and decidedly unmusical notes. These hadn't come from the band, however, but from the pier's superstructure, now creaking and groaning beneath us.

She finished to enthusiastic cheers from the Prothero clan and polite clapping from everyone else. I watched her take a couple of curtain calls, then walk off the stage. When she reached the wings she didn't stop, just kept walking. She could, of course, have been going to the ladies' loo for a quick repair job, but somehow I knew that she wasn't. There was something final about that exit.

I tried to catch Grady's eye. When I succeeded I jerked my head sideways, in the direction of the wings. She rose uncertainly to her feet. I jerked my head again and this time she got the message. As she made for the exit there came the sound of breaking glass and a curtain blew violently inward. The wind had broken a window-pane.

By now the storm outside the Pavilion was louder than the noise inside and our audience was fast losing its nerve. Already the two policemen were on their feet and even Ernie was looking apprehensive. As for

113

Neville, I could tell by the way he was sweating that his concentration was breaking up. He kept looking sideways to where Diamond had disappeared.

Suddenly he stopped beating time. The band went on playing, but I took my chance to leap off the podium and race through the wings to the door leading on to the pierhead. I flung it open and for a moment the force of the wind took my breath away. Reeling back, I tried to adjust my vision to the darkness.

Then I saw them. Two figures struggling by the rail.

Grady had managed to get an armlock around Diamond's neck. Sea spray pounded up from below, drenching them both, and as I went towards them the entire pierhead seemed to shift beneath my feet. It was this unexpected movement that gave Diamond a chance to break free. She thrust Grady aside, throwing her against me, and turned to run.

At that moment one of the policemen came round the corner to block her exit. She stopped dead. As Grady and I struggled upright the sound of the band petered out behind us in a discordant whimper.

Neville appeared from the stage door. "Di? Di, where are you?"

She didn't answer. Her eyes fixed on the advancing policeman, she began to back away.

But the other policeman had come round behind the Pavilion, cutting off her retreat. He called out something, the words lost in the wind. Alerted, Diamond swung round and saw him. In blind panic she dashed to the rail and began to climb over.

"Di, come back!" Neville yelled. "Don't be a fool."

At this point Ernie and the rest of the Protheros

arrived on the scene, but they all pulled up short when they saw what was happening. For the space of about two seconds we stood like a frozen video frame, watching the woman on the rail, while the wind howled and screeched round our ears.

I was the nearest. The realization came like a sickening blow. If anyone was going to make a move it had to be me. Cautiously I began to edge towards the rail. No one was looking at me, they were too busy staring at Diamond. And she was staring down at the heaving, angry sea beneath her with a kind of hypnotic fascination.

I'd almost reached her when there came an almighty crack and the boards beneath my feet gave way, throwing me forward. At the same instant the rail buckled and Diamond lost her balance, clawing wildly at the air. I reached out a hand to grab her, but it was too late: she'd already begun to fall. Horrified, I watched her dropping downwards, out of my sight.

I inched forward on my stomach until I could look over the edge, then saw that somehow she'd managed to catch hold of a wooden spar and was hanging on, suspended perilously over the churning sea. Her ghost-white face gazed up at me, desperately pleading. Holding on to what was left of the rail, I reached down to where her hand was clenched over the rotting wood, but suddenly the pier groaned again and I felt myself beginning to slide. Somebody grabbed my ankles and Grady's voice yelled, "Hang on, Mack! I've got you."

The groaning of the boards turned into a roar, and above the roar I heard splintering wood, followed by a woman's scream. It froze my bones, a chilling echo of the scream that had haunted me since I'd first heard it in the fog. But this time I had no doubt in my mind that it was Diamond.

Then came the splash.

If Grady hadn't kept a tight grip on me I'd have gone over as well, but somehow she managed to haul me to safety. We collapsed together in a heap at Ma's feet. When I looked round, part of the pier had disappeared and with it Diamond Jones. Bonnie hid her face against her father's chest. He seemed paralyzed and so did everyone else.

Everyone except Neville. With a yell of anguish he raced towards the gap in the railings and did what he hadn't had the courage to do when Joe Prince went over. He dived in after her.

Chapter Fifteen

Next morning, in the Seagull Caff, Grady and I sat facing the now deserted pier. It looked like a wounded seagull flying off-balance, with one wing missing. The entrance was boarded up and even as we watched a large notice was being erected saying DANGER, KEEP OUT.

"I reckon Ernie's in trouble," Grady said. "He should never have fixed up that show in the Pavilion. He must have known it was structurally unsafe. If the audience had been bigger . . ."

I shuddered and then winced. One of my ribs was cracked when I fell last night against the rail.

She went on, "Serve him right if he gets chucked off the Council. They've been waiting for him to make this kind of mistake for years."

"He'll bluff his way out of it," I said. "He always does. He'll probably appeal to their sympathies, on account of his sister being drowned."

"*If* she was drowned. We still don't know for

certain. After all, they could both swim, unlike Joe Prince."

"Nobody could survive in that sea. They didn't stand a chance." I glared at the crowd that had gathered on the esplanade, ghoulishly waiting for the bodies to be washed ashore. "I hate this. It isn't that I liked Diamond particularly, because I didn't, but she can't have been all bad or she wouldn't have inspired such devotion in poor old Neville. Whatever she'd done in the past he'd stuck by her – and tried to keep the band going at the same time. You've got to hand it to him."

Grady gave me a curious look. "You used not to be so pro-Neville."

"That's when I thought he was a murderer. Now I'm pretty sure he was just a hen-pecked husband. No wonder the Protheros didn't like him. He wasn't in their league."

Grady cleared her throat.

I saw she was looking at someone over my shoulder and swung round. Bonnie stood there, white-faced and sorrowful. "Oh, hi," I said, trying to sound as normal as possible. "Take a seat."

She sat. "I came to see how you were."

"I'm fine. Listen, I'm sorry about yesterday, but—"

"It's me that should be sorry. Mack, I'd no idea that Aunt Diamond had murdered someone. Truly, you've got to believe me."

I said, "Bonnie, she didn't murder anyone. It was self-defence. Joe Prince tried to strangle her."

"I don't mean Joe Prince. I mean the man she shot five years ago during a poker game."

I stared at her incredulously. Grady, who'd been on the point of getting up, sat down again.

"It was a kind of accident," Bonnie went on. "She always carried a gun in her handbag, just a little one, in case of trouble. Then she got annoyed with this man—"

"Why, did he accuse her of cheating?"

"No, he was rude about her singing voice."

Clearly Diamond, too, had her professional pride. "How did she get away with it?"

"She pleaded self-defence, said the man had threatened her physically. Uncle Neville backed her up and so did Joe Prince. He was one of the players."

And had been bleeding them dry ever since for hush money. So that's what Diamond had meant about her record, if it came to a second trial. A plea of self-defence might have worked the first time around, but not if she looked like making a habit of it.

"So she got off scot-free?"

"No, she was found guilty of manslaughter. They sent her to jail, but only for eighteen months."

Long enough for her to decide she didn't want to risk being sent back. "How do you know all this?" I asked Bonnie.

"Kevin told me." She added in a small voice, "I guess she wasn't a very nice person, Mack. That's why I don't blame you for not wanting to have anything to do with me."

"You think that's why I walked out on you?" I said, amazed. "But it had nothing to do with that. I went because I thought Olive Pilling was in danger."

"It's okay." She put a hand on my arm. "You don't have to make excuses. I understand." She glanced at Grady, who was looking equally incredulous. "I'd better go."

As she stood up I said quickly, "Bonnie, wait. I'd like to make it up to you for yesterday. Are you doing anything this evening?"

"I'm leaving today. Dad thinks it's best." She gave me a sad little smile. "You could write to me, Mack. I'd like that. Maybe I can persuade Mom to let me come again, for a longer visit next time. 'Bye now. It's been real nice knowing you."

"It's been nice knowing you too." I watched her go, then turned to Grady. "Can you please explain to me how a sweet, innocent kid like that could possibly be a Prothero?"

She shrugged. "Nature plays strange tricks."

Something in her tone, a trace of scepticism, made me ask, "You don't think she's genuine?"

"Oh, she's genuine enough. Nobody could keep up that Scarlett O'Hara act for days on end unless it was for real."

I looked at her hard. "You disapprove?"

"Of you, not her. I never saw you looking lovesick before, Mack. It doesn't suit you."

"I suppose you think it's a sign of weakness?"

"Let's just say I like you better when you're being your normal intolerant self." She nodded at the door. "The way you are with her, for instance."

I groaned as I saw Jennifer Wainwright enter, her eyes – one of them now turning greenish-yellow – raking the caff like searchlights. As soon as she spotted me she came over. "Mack, I've got something to tell you."

I stood up. "Not now, Jennifer, I'm leaving."

"It's about that person who bumped into me." Her face was flushed with self-importance. "You remember. In the fog."

My feet froze to the floor. "Go on."

"Well, it happened again last night. I was coming to see you at the Pavilion, you see, only Mum wouldn't let me out so I had to climb through the window and that's why I was late. But I was running along the esplanade when suddenly wham, he knocked me over."

"He?"

"I knew it was the same man because he smelled funny. And guess what, Mack, he was dripping wet. Do you think I should go to the police?" She gazed at me with the eager triumph of a dog returning a stick to its master.

I said coldly, "You're making it up, Jennifer. How could a man smell of perfume after he'd been in the water?"

"I didn't say it was perfume. More sort of . . . seaweedy."

"Sorry, I don't believe you. Go to the police if you want, but you'd better be sure and tell them the truth, otherwise you'll be in dead trouble."

She subsided like a spent tyre. "But, Ma-ack . . ."

"Come on," I said to Grady. "Let's go."

Outside Grady said, "You think that was just a bid for your attention?"

"Don't you? So convenient, just after she'd heard of the drownings, to bump into someone who's dripping wet. The story doesn't hold water – if you'll pardon the expression." When we reached the Honda I said, "Any chance of a lift?"

"Sorry. I promised Olive I'd take her out for a run. She wants me to do a ton down the M27. She's a game girl, old Olive. Did you know she once owned a Douglas?"

"Yeah, I did. Give her my love. Oh, and Grady – I don't believe I ever thanked you properly for saving my life last night. If you hadn't grabbed me—"

"Say another word, MacBride, and I'll ram that

121

fatal charm of yours right down your throat!"

I grinned appreciatively. Good old Grade.

I arrived back at the hotel to see a familiar blue Mercedes parked outside. Puzzled, I watched as first Ernie came down the steps, then Wild Bill and Georgie, all carrying suitcases. "Hey," I demanded. "What's going on?"

Ernie, grim-faced, ignored me. Wild Bill muttered, "Keep out of our way, Snoopy."

I raced up the steps to reach the door just as Kevin came out, carrying yet another suitcase, and charged through to the reception desk, where Ma was presiding with Junoesque calm. "They're removing all the Brands' belongings," I panted. "Is that legal?"

She shrugged. "I told Ernie Prothero he was welcome to take them. After all they did belong to his sister."

"But what about the police? Won't they need the stuff as evidence?"

"Evidence of what? The case is closed as far as they're concerned."

"How can it be closed until they find the bodies?"

"They already have," Ma said. "At least, they found one of them. It was washed ashore about three miles up the coast."

I went cold. "Which one?"

"The woman." Ma's tone softened. "Don't look like that, Nigel. It's been a nasty business, especially last night on the pier. You had a bad experience. But now you have to put it behind you and get on with life." She added more bracingly, "Such as helping your father in the kitchen. So far this weekend you haven't exactly pulled your weight, so perhaps now's a good time to start?"

They never did find Neville Brand's body, which made me wonder if Jennifer Wainwright had been telling the truth after all. Perhaps I'd been wrong to stop her going to the police. Not that I lost any sleep over it. As I'd said to Grady, the poor guy couldn't have had an easy life with Diamond, no matter how much he'd loved her. Maybe somewhere, sometime, he'd manage to set up another version of the Blue City Swingers, this time with a more harmonious vocalist. I wished him luck, I really did.

As long as the drummer wasn't me.